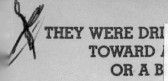

THEY WERE DRI
TOWARD
OR A B

Cotton Dunbar: The tall man with steely blue eyes lost everything while he was fighting a war. Now, he was fighting for a new life—and living by the only rules he'd ever learned.

Ardie Rousseau: The affable Louisiana Cajun had a habit of making jokes when things got rough. But beneath the clown was a wounded heart, an iron will, and the best man Cotton had ever known.

Penny Dickinson: The young widow tended to Cotton's house after the murder of his family. Cheerful despite the hardships she'd faced, she was the kind of woman who could make a man want to start over.

Mr. Oglethorpe: "My word is good and my bank is sound," the Abilene banker told Cotton when he contracted to buy his cattle. For Cotton, the agreement meant everything.

"JACK CURTIS'S SPARE STYLE AND SHARP EYE FOR CHARACTER WILL KEEP HIS BOOKS FRESH WELL INTO THE COMING CENTURY."
—Loren D. Estleman

Look for Jack Curtis's:
The Sheriff Kill
Available from Pocket Books
and
Blood Cut
Coming soon from Pocket Books

Books by Jack Curtis

The Sheriff Kill
Texas Rules

Published by POCKET BOOKS

JACK CURTIS

TEXAS RULES

POCKET BOOKS

New York   London   Toronto   Sydney   Tokyo   Singapore

An *Original* Publication of POCKET BOOKS

POCKET BOOKS, a division of Simon & Schuster
1230 Avenue of the Americas, New York, NY 10020

ISBN: 0-671-67274-6

First Pocket Books printing June 1991

10 9 8 7 6 5 4 3 2 1

POCKET and colophon are registered trademarks of
Simon & Schuster.

Cover art copyright by Lino Saffioti

Printed in the U.S.A.

TEXAS RULES

--**1**----------

A northern breeze hummed across the grassy hillside, riffling the pretty bluebonnets that grew most thickly in a small oval-shaped depression. A bow of light spring steel, still sewn with a tatter of yellow taffeta, arched a few inches over the sunken grave.

Maybe they'd mounded it over when they buried her and the boy, but the winds and rains had exposed that part of her best Sunday dress.

The way they told it, Donna and the boy and the old vaquero, Lupe, were driving the wagon down to Dickinson's ranch on a Sunday morning for the christening of all the babies in the countryside.

They had meant to have a potluck dinner afterward.

A stray band of Comanches cut them off. When Lupe was riven with arrows and pitched aside, Donna had tried to make a run for it. They'd speared her and the boy right here and rode off with the team and wagon.

Donna was twenty, and the boy would have been four in May.

Next day the folks came up from Dickinson's and buried what was left. With the Indians still about and hot for blood, you couldn't fault those folks for hurrying the grave.

But inside that hoop under the bluebonnets, only a few inches away, was everything Cotton Dunbar had lived for.

In all the years of killing up and down the land from Bull Run to Appomattox, Cotton Dunbar had kept his big jaw solid, his teeth locked, his blue eyes dry as desert frost, but the partially buried frivolous hoop, that pathetic remnant of her femininity, tore a great sobbing groan from his chest. Burying his rocky face in his arms, he let the flood of sorrow break out of his heart.

All this was his fault! This gentle scene of sleeping waste and horror came about because he'd gone off to fight Yankees instead of staying by his family.

No matter that he'd thought the Comanches were long gone, no matter that he'd believed the war would be over by spring, it was his mistake that had permitted such a black Sunday morning just a year ago.

No matter that he'd been hit at Five Forks and lay more dead than alive for months afterward, or that he'd willed that he must live to return to his family; though by then they were already here, and he thought now it would have been better if he'd given up and died, than to return to this sorry hill.

From what seemed a far distance away, he heard Ardie's gentle voice. "Let it be, Captain, let it be."

He felt Ardie's hand on his bowed-over shoulder, and knew that whatever happened, he had to go on. If there was any give-up in him, it would have surfaced a long time before. He swallowed his tears and cleared his throat.

Ardie Rousseau, standing close by, said, "I'll come back later and fix it proper."

The big man, Cotton Dunbar, set his jaw, rose to his feet and whispered, "I'd appreciate that, Ardie."

"But tomorrow?" his battle-forged comrade asked as they walked to their horses. "You want to come along west?"

"No, friend, I'm going to put this back together best I can."

Ardie Rousseau's reputation for being comical in godawful hard times was of no use to him here. A lanky, dark-haired man with a Cajun's mobile face, Ardie rarely admitted despondency, because any kind of a joke was better, even if you didn't believe in it. It was his own way of carrying on.

But there could be no levity on this lonely hillside, and he said, "Maybe you'd be better putting it all behind, like me."

"Yours was burned and scavenged by carpetbaggers. The ranch is still here. The cattle have increased fourfold, and I made a promise."

"There's no one left to hold you to any promise."

"There's neighbors that helped her, and you can bet they're needing help right now."

Riding across the bottom flat toward the cotton-woods that marked the ranch house, Ardie studied the lay of the low hills, the broken-down picket fences, the rotted haystack, the barn and sheds that showed the decrepitude of neglect, and lastly, the low ranch house with its summer veranda and dog run between the living part and sleeping part. The boards were warping apart for lack of paint. The roof needed new shakes, and cattle had rubbed the gate post down.

Still, the neighbors, mainly Penny Dickinson, had kept the doors secure, and inside, the floor was clean and things tidied up.

Penny had told Cotton when they first stopped by that she'd thought it best to put all of Donna's things in the steamer trunk in case of rats.

Cotton said nothing when he saw the big tin trunk in the bedroom corner, and he held his peace when he saw the quilt with the shooting star pattern and the name Donna Dunbar embroidered in the corner. Probably the trunk was too full to hold any more. No one opened it up to look.

Ardie went into the kitchen to the hand pump on the sink, unscrewed the handle, and carried the piston with its dried-up leather washers out to the stone spring house, where he set the leather to soaking.

Cotton met Ardie on the veranda, his hard-lined face shaped back into its usual impervious granite. "Care to stay on?"

"I was thinking of heading on west and soaking my sore backsides in the Pacific Ocean."

"Saltwater's no good for nothing."

"I guess you really mean it."

"Wouldn't hurt to try. No hard feelings if you feel like drifting on."

"Gosh, Cotton, I told Maybelle I'd be home before dark." Ardie laughed, showing strong white teeth as he rollicked on about his imaginary sweetheart. "She gets mighty upset if I have to tiptoe in carrying my boots."

"You'll have to show her who's boss." Cotton smiled.

"Ever try to tell a striped tiger crossed on a grizzly bear sow that you're boss?"

"I'm right glad you're staying," Cotton said, "but we don't have all day for palavering about your Maybelle."

"Where do we start?"

"First thing we're going to need is a stout horse corral where we can buck out some of the wild ones."

Ardie's clown face puckered up in mock dismay. "I hear a man can get his aitch bone bucked up around his ears that way. Maybe we ought to carve some splints and crutches first."

That evening, before turning in, Cotton started a list of supplies they needed. Building materials, groceries, a wagon, and maybe a team of mules.

"What are we using for money?" Ardie asked.

"Sure not these shin plasters." Cotton tossed a thick bundle of hundred-dollar Confederate bills on the table. "I reckon first I better find out who our local banker is."

In the morning, on the trail to Tres Cruces, Cotton stopped by Widow Dickinson's ranch. Like his Bar D, it was nestled up against a northern slope and overlooked a bottomland through which a small creek meandered. The house was similar to his but lacked the special details that he had lavished on his own.

Penny Dickinson, small and erect, still young despite the hardness of her life, came down the front steps to meet him.

She wore a clean gingham frock and comfortable short boots to work in. Her long russet hair was tied up under a straw hat, and her freckled face was alive and cheerful with good health and plain thinking.

Married young, she and her husband Tom had

pioneered the ranch shortly after Cotton and Donna had settled in the valley to the north.

They'd all gotten along fine until the day Tom tore his thumb on a rusty horseshoe nail. In a week the strong young man was dead of blood poison.

She looked up and studied Cotton's face for signs of a crack-up, and seeing none, smiled and said, "Come in, neighbor, and have some coffee."

Stacey, her flaxen-haired younger brother, followed down the steps and shook hands with Cotton. Scarcely seventeen, he was not much taller than Penny and not likely to grow more. His eyes were shaped like Penny's, but the deep blue of her eyes was thinned out to almost silver in his. With his white eyebrows and pale, washed-out eyes, there was something missing, something important, but hard to put your finger on.

Odd, Cotton thought, you'd never know they was even kin.

Over coffee he thanked her for keeping the ranch house secure and taking care of things for him.

"I'm afraid we couldn't keep tally on your herd, Cotton," she said, "but you've got a good crop of longhorns in the brush."

Something stirred in his chest as she spoke. Something about her open, cheerful face, her graceful figure. Or was it just the smell of fresh gingham? He put the vague feeling aside. She was his wife's friend and a good neighbor, that's all there ever would be to it.

"Reckon you better catch 'em before you sell 'em," Stacey said. "Those critters are faster'n rabbits and a hundred times meaner."

"Who would buy them?" Cotton asked.

"That's where the saddle slips. Nobody around here wants them." Penny smiled.

"Much obliged to you for everything, Penny," Cotton said, getting to his feet. "Let me know if me and Ardie can be of help."

"Ardie's staying on with you?" she asked.

"Long as he wants. A few years ago he was a fancy dandy on a rich plantation. When he got home, the big house was burned and all his people dead and gone. He's kind of like a man left over from a shipwreck right now, just floating along until he can get his bearings back."

Cotton tipped his hat and left.

There were other ranches along the way, but he didn't stop. There would be time enough later on. Besides, he wasn't running for office, and a lot of these folks had better things to do than set around talking about hard times.

If Tres Cruces wasn't the county seat it might not even be there, Cotton speculated as he rode down the dusty main street and saw no signs of improvement over the last time he'd seen it. The bank on the main corner was built of quarried stone, but the rest of the businesses were constructed of rough-sawn lumber. Paint was peeling. The gingerbread gewgaws on the false fronts sagged, and the town looked just plain dirty with piles of horse manure and a dead dog baiting a blanket of flies.

What had once been a large Mexican adobe ranch house had been taken over for the county courthouse, while the population lived in small houses scattered about without regard to street boundaries.

The only thing new in town was a telegraph office next to the livery stable.

The saloons didn't attract him, and he rode directly to the hitchrack in front of the bank.

The First National seemed like every country bank he'd ever been in, the folks whispering and looking mournful. The clerk behind the grill, with his black armlets protecting his starched shirt, murmured to an old woman as if he was suggesting an assignation at a funeral, and the air smelled dead as last week.

"Hello, sir," came a hearty voice.

Turning left, Cotton Dunbar saw a big, rotund robin of a man dressed in a dark suit with a gold chain across his vest. He showed a mouthful of teeth in a clenched smile, his face rigid, his eyes cold as hailstones.

"Good morning," Cotton offered.

"Can I be of service? My name's Julius Hightower. Take a chair."

Cotton sat in a hard wooden chair across from the banker and explained his situation.

"And your assets consist of three sections of land in Eldorado County?"

"It's some improved," Cotton said. "And there's a couple thousand head of cows out there, too."

"I can't loan money on cows in the brush. Fact is, around here a prime steer wouldn't bring two dollars. Other fact is, money's tight."

Money's always tight every time you see a banker, Cotton thought, but you got to listen to his calf splatter if you want the money.

"I only need enough to patch up the ranch until there's a market for beef."

By putting up the land as collateral, Cotton finally got a little money at a very high rate of interest. The loan wasn't anything near the worth of the land, but given a couple of months breathing time, Cotton thought he could have steers on the market and clear the note.

It was true there wasn't any money left. Only the bankers coming down from the north with a carpetbag full of war profits could put out any real cash, and that was natural, Cotton realized, same as buzzards always turn up when some fine animal starves to death.

The South had spent it all, their money, their blood, their way of life, and that was the way such a fight ought to end. Because if you lost because you were half-hearted, you'd have lost your pride too. They had given the war everything there was, and for that the South at least had kept its pride. Not the pride of plumed hats and cigars dipped in old bourbon, but the simple pride of a straight back and steady eyes, beholden to no man.

Late in the evening he drove the wagon into the yard, loaded with supplies and trailing his riding horse.

"Hello the house," Cotton shouted.

Need a dog, he thought for a second, and then the broad boistery of Ardie's voice quieted his fears.

"That you, Maybelle? I swear, honey, I'm all alone and ain't smoked a cigareet, touched whiskey, or contemplated the hem of a skirt . . ."

"Just fetch in the staples the varmints might want. We can get the rest of it later," Cotton said, worn-out from spending a day borrowing money and spending it.

While Ardie unloaded the wagon, Cotton unhitched the mules and put them in the temporary corral for the night.

Next morning, with wire and spikes and leftover

timbers, they made the horse corral tight and permanent. Cotton dragged a log in from the creek bottom and they set it four feet deep in the center of the corral for a snubbin' post.

In a week's time they had the main holding pasture in the creek bottom fenced tightly and they were ready for business.

"You ready to buck brush?" Cotton asked after their evening meal of fried beef and boiled beans.

"I laced up some armor for my horse and for myself out of an old cowhide. I guess it'll limber up in time."

Cotton nodded. "Time you tear through a batch of chollas and creeping devil, you'll be glad it's tough."

He was satisfied with their progress. Of course, the country was overdue for a good rain, but all they needed now was to gather the cattle and horses gone wild, and they'd have a working ranch. No reason why they couldn't pay off the banker early.

He wanted to get the land clear again. Something about that banker's smile gave him the williwaws.

When he paid off that troublesome mortgage, he'd have it all back the way it was, except ... Except there was no way, even as big and determined as he was, no way to bring Donna back. He hardly knew the boy, he was more like a wishing dream than a real child in Cotton's mind. But his memories of Donna were real enough to make him shudder in the night.

To forget those visions, Cotton drove himself all the harder, with never a day of rest, although he tried not to force his fanatic drive onto Ardie, who had his own ruined dreams to forget by playacting with the invisible Maybelle.

"Maybelle, by golly, you sure are a dream girl of a

cook! What I mean, you can burn beans just right every time," he bantered with himself at the iron cookstove. Or chasing steers and popping brush, he'd call out, "Maybelle, I'd love you more if'n your legs was some less prickly, and you left the rattlesnakes out'n the bed . . ."

Cotton thought if it would just rain some they'd have a chance, shading his eyes under the sweat-stained Stetson, trying to see a wary renegade steer through the parched mesquite. The critters had learned to hide better than catamounts on their own, and they could outrun a good horse in the spiny, jagged vegetation, and they'd fight a man if cornered.

Only way to bring them in was to outsmart them, and turn their flanks same as Lee herded the Yankee generals until Grant and Sherman just said they didn't want to play fox and hounds, they just wanted a straight up-and-down slaughterhouse. They had the more blood to waste.

But that was on east where it rained and the grass grew hip deep. Here was the land of brutal sun and long shadow. Here was a drab, spiny, dwarfed jungle that would not carry a raven except for a trace of dew.

There had been no appreciable rain in two years, Cotton learned, and it meant they had to suffer through a drought on top of everything else.

Cotton kneed his gelding and charged the brush. His bluff sent a tiger-striped bull charging away down the coulee, where it would find more docile company and maybe stay around until Ardie and he could move them along into the bottom pasture, where there was still good feed and a rough-hewn gate that would hold them in the gather.

In a month he and Ardie had bunched up a couple hundred good beeves that ought to be enough to settle the note and then some. All he needed was a buyer.

"We've not had any luck," Penny said when he stopped by. "The buyers used to come out here, but now we have to go looking."

"I'm not asking much," Cotton said. "Just clear my debt and then set my sights on bringing the ranch up to standard."

"You ought to take a little time off. Maybe we could organize a picnic down in the pecan grove, bring all us scrabbling folks together for just a good time."

"Not yet, Penny. One thing at a time. I won't feel right until I sell that stock."

"Later, then." She smiled, and he dipped his hat and rode on alone into Tres Cruces.

He could find no one interested in buying cattle. He rode north and came into old San Antonio the next day. He didn't look for a barber or a bath, he looked for a beef buyer. But the corral outside the slaughterhouse was already full of beef cattle, and he was told those cattle had been bought for two dollars a head.

If they had a railroad, sure, they could ship the beef east to where the people were next to starving, but there was no railroad closer than Kansas.

Sitting on the top rail of the stockyard fence with a group of other cattlemen, Cotton listened to the slow conversation.

". . . 'course there was talk of driving herds up John Chisholm's trail to Kansas . . . They say there's a man from Kansas taking orders right now . . . he's staying in the Cattleman's Hotel."

Cotton drifted away toward the center of town and found the two-story brick hotel on the main street.

The man at the desk pointed out a stocky businessman in a blue suit. He was seated in the lobby, going
through a sheaf of papers.

"That's Mr. Oglethorpe."

The stocky man glanced up irritably, as if wishing
not to be disturbed, when Cotton came up to him and
said, "Pardon me. Mr. Oglethorpe?"

"Yes?"

"You buying cattle?"

"Sit down. Your name?"

"Cotton Dunbar, from out northwest of Tres Cruces," Cotton said, studying the man who might be the
difference between winning or losing for him. He
didn't like what he saw, the softness, the slight cast of
one eye, the stink of the cigar, and the northern, quick
clip to his voice.

"I have a bank in Abilene, Kansas, a fine up-and-
coming town with a brand new railroad called the
Hannibal and St. Joseph. Soon as it's finished, that
railroad will haul beef to the eastern markets and
make us all some money. Understand what I mean?"

"You buying beef?"

"I'm contracting for beef to be delivered to Abilene
this summer."

"How many do you want?"

"I'll buy all you can bring." Oglethorpe laughed
smugly.

"Are you putting up a bond?"

"I don't have to. My word is good and my bank
sound. I'll write you a contract, and when the time's
right, I'll send a message. If you don't want to bring
your herd north, well, you can—" Noting the hardness in Cotton's frosty eyes, Oglethorpe didn't finish
his sentence. Instead he changed his manner into that

13

of an affable, big-hearted businessman. "There's no problem, Mr. Dunbar. The only problem is from here to there, and that's your job."

"Your price, sir?"

"The latest market price from the east coast is thirty-three dollars a head for prime stock delivered."

"If you'll write that up, I'll start working up a herd."

Oglethorpe didn't like Cotton Dunbar, his steadiness or his tenacity, yet that's the way these Texas ranchers were. They didn't like to make a lot of talk and play the game, they just wanted something solid to bite down on, and leave it at that.

Quickly Oglethorpe filled out a printed form that promised to buy all the cattle Cotton could bring for thirty-three dollars a head, depending only on receiving firm confirmation that the railhead was ready and waiting for the herd.

"I don't want any misunderstandings, Mr. Oglethorpe," Cotton said softly to the pudgy banker. "Is there anything else I need to know?"

"Gather your cattle, Mr. Dunbar." Oglethorpe grinned, showing a rack of yellow teeth. "Time's awasting."

2

Sitting on the front steps in the cool of the evening, Cotton tried to explain to Ardie the impossibility of selling the cattle in Tres Cruces.

"What do you suppose that banker will want next after he swallers up south Texas?" Ardie asked. "My Maybelle?"

"A tapeworm never stops," Cotton said.

"But you been quiet as a tree full of owls since you got back. Why don't you just 'fess up you found a new cook in San Antone?"

"Here it is." Cotton smiled, glad to get it off his chest. "There's a man, a Kansas banker, buying cattle in San Antone. He's paying thirty-three dollars a head for grade beef."

"Bye, bye, Maybelle! I'll be back soon as I spend some money!" Ardie sang out with joy.

"It's not that easy. First we need to deliver the critters to Abilene, Kansas."

15

Ardie's smile faded. "That's better'n a thousand miles . . ."

"It's the nearest railhead. Only John Chisholm ever done it, and he didn't like it."

"That banker keep his promise?"

"He gave me a paper that guaranteed the price."

"How many?"

"I told him we might make up a herd of ours and the neighbors, maybe put a couple thousand head together."

"I'm ready, Captain," Ardie said, seriously for a change.

"Tomorrow I'll ride over to Dickinson's, and you get word to the neighbors to meet us over there."

"Oh my, oh my, if you ain't just as calm as a horse trough." Ardie smiled.

"You know on north there's still some Injuns loose, and there's plenty of roughnecks left over from the war that would like a piece of free cake."

"Sure, and there's rain and hail, thunder and lightning, rattlesnakes and scorpions. I didn't hear you say it'd be easy."

"Just so everybody knows."

In the morning Cotton rode over to the Dickinson ranch and was met at the gate by Penny, fresh and perky as ever. Her shoebutton eyes, alight with mischief, gazed up at Cotton's rock-hard features.

"C'mon, Cotton," she said, offering her cheek, "give me a neighborly kiss."

"Ma'am?" Cotton stammered.

"You can do it," she teased, "if you bend down a little."

Cotton flushed and pecked her freckled cheek with dry lips.

16

"Not bad for a starter." She grinned. "Come inside, the coffeepot's on and there's prune cake in the pantry."

Young Stacey rose from the table and shook hands while Penny poured the coffee and served the cake.

"Settle down," she said firmly, "and tell us some good news."

Cotton explained that there would be others arriving soon, and when everyone had gathered, he wanted to talk about his trip to San Antonio.

"I wish I could have gone along," Stacey said. "I'd like to do something different for a change."

Before Cotton could reply, Penny heard the call of visitors outside and went to welcome the neighbors to the west.

Old Deef had taken up his ground in the coulee country just to be alone. He had some cattle but was eating jackrabbit.

Cash Pardee's land lay in between Dickinson's and Old Deef's. He'd taken a ball in the neck at Stone Mountain and couldn't turn his head without turning his whole bulky body.

Both men, with weather-bitten faces and sun-checked eyes, walked with the hobbling gait common to men accustomed to riding.

When they were all settled down at the kitchen table, Cotton explained the problem and how he hoped to solve it.

"I heard somewhere that Colonel Goodnight tried it last year and come back with his saddlebags stuffed with greenbacks." Cash Pardee nodded. "You can count me in."

"Me, too," Old Deef said. He could hear as good as anyone when he wanted.

"There'll be others from across the valley," Penny added, "to help make up the herd."

"I figure ten drovers, a wrangler, and a cookhand. If the owners can't go, they can send a couple of their top hands."

"I can go," Stacey put in quickly.

"It'll be hard enough for a grown man, Stacey," Penny worried. "Maybe you should wait till next year."

"I said I was going," Stacey replied angrily. "I'm not a kid anymore."

"All right," Penny said quietly, "but I want to send Juan along as the wrangler, too. He's the best."

"I got nobody to send and not all that many cows," Old Deef put in, "but I do fancy them Kansas jackrabbits a sight more than the homegrown variety."

"I'd never make it." Cash Pardee wanted to shake his head, but all he could do was sway back and forth. "But I'll send along my best riders."

"Talk it over with Block Diamond and the Martin brothers," Cotton said. "There's not much time for setting on a fence rail making chin music."

"What all will we need?" Stacey asked.

"Say about fifty horses, a chuckwagon, plenty of the best guns, and a lot of luck."

"You can borrow my cook, Kelly, if you promise to bring him back." Cash smiled. "He's blacker'n sin, but nobody can touch his corn dodgers and sowbelly."

"Can he stand the ride?" Stacey asked coolly.

"I'd ride anywhere with him and rest easy at night, too," Cash responded.

"All right," Cotton said, "I'm setting the date. Come hell or high water we're aimin' for Abilene April fifteenth."

—————————————————————— **3** ——

On the night of April tenth, when most of the cattle had been road branded and the extra horses brought down to the Dickinson's ranch, Cotton and Ardie were awakened by the clattering of hooves outside and Stacey Dickinson's cry, "They've stoled the horses!"

"Good gracious all to hell, Maybelle," Ardie called out, while Cotton put on his hat and then lighted the lamp. "You like to scared me loose from my hair."

Mounting spooky horses in the night, with saddle leather popping and the horses grunting, Cotton listened to Stacey's excited report.

"Wasn't Indians, was Mexicans, the old man said when we found him. They got a three-hour head start, and they're heading south for the border. I was goin' after 'em by myself, but Penny lost her temper."

"That's a wise lady," Cotton said. "How many you figure?"

"Old Enrique thought there was four or five."

"Heck, if there's only five, we might as well go on back to the bunkhouse and let old Stacey here take care of them."

Cotton understood well enough that the hotheaded youth was wild and untried, and he didn't smile at Ardie's teasing. He reckoned if the kid got himself hurt, Penny would never forgive him.

Going on a dead run straight south meant they were trailing Mexicans from across the big river. For sure, they knew their own ground.

They weren't trying to hide their trail, because they meant to make a quick dash back across the border to safety.

At least they hadn't killed the old man on guard. They reckoned he'd stay tied up all night, a bad mistake.

Still, he respected them for showing him some mercy.

At dawn the tracks of the running herd were plain but there was no dust cloud up ahead.

"It means they've crossed the river or they're holed up," Cotton muttered.

On they rode through the parched land, broken by low hills.

Coming to the crest of one of those hills, Cotton raised his hand and pulled his sweating mount to a halt.

"If they're just over this hill, we don't want to spook them," he said. "If they're not down there, then they've beat us."

"We can cross over the river after 'em," Stacey declared.

"Sure, but the odds get worse with every mile, and we'll study that when we have to."

"Maybelle always told me to stay out of foreign countries," Ardie whispered.

"Let's go. Quiet . . ."

Stopping at the crest of the next hill, they saw the remains of an abandoned Mexican rancho down below. The adobe buildings were in ruins, but there was water and the herd of horses were drinking. To one side the rustlers had built a small fire for a quick breakfast of tortillas and melted cheese and chili.

"Now we caught the tiger, what're we goin' to do with it?" Ardie smiled.

"Charge," Stacey said impatiently.

"We ought to be some smarter'n that," Cotton said. "See how that coulee to the west forks around the ranch? Ardie, you take the near fork and hold it when we come up out of the far one."

"Yes, Captain." Ardie tossed a mock salute. "We're goin' whip 'em singlehanded, Maybelle," he added to himself.

They split up at the brushy fork, Ardie going left, Cotton and Stacey taking the right.

"Now listen to me, son," Cotton said when he judged they were even with the rancho yard, "we're not goin' in there blazing. We're goin' in so quiet they won't know it until too late. I don't want you to fire that Colt unless it's life or death, understand?"

Stacey stared at him in wonder. Was this the great cavalryman who'd fought Sheridan to a standstill? Had he gotten too old and feeble to make a fight?

"Understood?" Cotton repeated steadily.

"I reckon, but it don't make sense."

"Whatever you do, don't get ahead of me."

Ground-tying their horses, they crept uphill through the brush to a crumbling adobe wall where they could hear the Mexicans speaking softly, probably discussing the weather, or their aches and pains, just like everybody else.

One quick look and Cotton saw that four men and a boy were gathered about the fire heating their tortillas on an old piece of tin.

"Manos arriba!" Cotton snapped as he came around the wall and faced them with a revolver in either hand.

The Mexicans, stunned by the suddenness of the catastrophe, were frozen for a moment in Cotton's vision, shreds of hot, rolled-up tortillas in their teeth.

Before they could turn, or draw, or run, Ardie said to their backs, *"Buenos días, señores."*

Their leader, a large man with graying hair, let his shoulders slump. "Please," he said in halting English, "someone steal our horses. We only take them back."

"Them horses never been yours," Cotton said. "You took the wrong bunch."

"In the dark, all horses look the same." The older man tried to smile, making the joke, shrugging his shoulders.

"Ordinarily we just hang horse thieves without any palavering," Cotton said.

"We are five against your three. I don't think you can hang anybody." The older man sighed. "Take back your horses and we will cross the river."

"Why'd you stop here? You could have beat us," Cotton asked, realizing these men were cowboys and ranchers much like himself. They weren't just ordinary scummy horse thieves out for a fast dollar to throw away in a bordertown saloon.

"This very place, this rancho, is my family home," the old man said. "All of this land for many miles was granted by the King of Spain to my family. Your armies came, and what they didn't take, they burned. I stop here because I am a sentimental man."

"Fight, Papa," the boy said fiercely.

"Quiet, *hijo,*" the old man murmured gently.

"Take their guns, Stacey," Cotton said, and to the older man, "It's the way it is. We don't want to have to be looking backward on the way home. Another time I hope we can be more friendly."

As Cotton spoke, he wanted to believe right was right, but he couldn't figure out who was a hundred percent right. He knew all about burned and destroyed ranches and plantations. He'd seen the desolate ruin of Ardie's home. He knew the heartfelt anguish at senseless destruction, and he was sorry for every family who'd ever lost their home to an army, but these were his horses and he meant to trail them back north and keep them.

Thinking and remembering, he let his attention ease off until Ardie spoke too late, "Stacey, don't get 'twixt them and Cotton!"

Sure enough, instead of going behind, Stacey was coming across in front, and just as Stacey blocked off the big man, the impetuous boy sprang at him with a small knife.

Even then they could have saved the whole trouble if Stacey had just backed off, but Stacey wasn't one to back up, and even as the old man and Cotton together were both yelling, "No! No! No!" Stacey quick-snapped his trigger, the bullet catapulting the kid off his feet.

After that split second there was no way to stop the hell that they were doing to themselves.

24

The older man stood straight as he drew. He had to draw and so did his men, because they didn't know what Stacey was going to do next. Knowing that Cotton had them in his sights and that another seasoned gunfighter was behind them, they instinctively reacted against Stacey, and for Cotton's part, he could not let Stacey be harmed even if he was stupid and deserved some punishment.

No way out. No right or wrong. Once more the scene of guns blazing and the air stinking sharply with burned powder and the unwanted screams of men dying.

Cotton held back until the last moment and shot the older man in the right shoulder, turned and caught a fleeing vaquero in the ribs and another in the chest. Ardie was adding his own deadly fire, and Stacey cut a swath, fanning the hammer of his revolver and forcing Ardie to duck for cover.

The old man dropped like a rock, although Cotton had wanted to save his life, whatever life he would have left after they'd finished. But there were too many fast-firing revolvers, and it was all too quick for thinking or for mercy. Once the first hammer dropped, there was no way of stopping the battle for survival.

As he looked at each ripped and sprawled body, Cotton saw that two of the vaqueros were unarmed, were too poor to own a gun.

"We whipped 'em!" Stacey yelled.

Cotton stared at the hot-blooded youth coldly and said, "Stupid."

"What do you mean? The kid went after me! Even hooked my shirt!"

"You ain't the first one to make a bad move," Cotton said, "but I hope you learned not to make another."

"They was horse thieves!" Stacey persisted, still high on fresh, smoking blood. "A barrelful of rattlesnakes."

"Maybelle always told me never to shoot nothing in a barrel because for sure you're going to ruin your barrel," Ardie said softly, stepping in between Cotton and Stacey. "Now likely these folks have kin closeby. Maybe we better just light a shuck north."

Cotton swallowed his revulsion and nodded silently.

"What's this all about!" Stacey yelled angrily. "They was just Mexicans!"

"You're sure right, Stacey." Cotton let his breath out slowly. "But what are they now?"

4

Cotton spoke gentle enough to the men, and he didn't spur blood out of his horse's shoulders, and he didn't cuss much, but he was coming to a boil.

They had put the herd together on the holding ground on the lower end of the Dickinson ranch where there was good water and new grass.

He had taken something like fifteen hundred head in little bunches from his neighbors and throwed in five hundred of his own, all he and Ardie could catch in a hurry. They were all road-branded, and along with eight cowpunchers, a cook on the chuckwagon, and a Mexican wrangler handling about fifty horses, ready to move. They were all set to drive north, excepting Dunbar wanted Oglethorpe's word from his Abilene, Kansas, bank that the deal was made like he said it would be.

Cotton sat his horse, working his big hands across the latigo-laced saddle horn, studying the dust of a

Jack Curtis

rider coming up from the south. Could be anybody,
but he was thinking it'd be Oglethorpe's rep. It had to
be him or they were going to have to drift the herd
west for more grass.

Behind him was the herd, tended by four cowpunchers, and camp where the rest were taking the
buck out of the greenest horses.

He thought of Penny for a moment. Was she put out
with him for scolding her kid brother? Were the
ranchers sorry they'd thrown in with him? Little
thoughts like that nagged at him as he waited for the
rider to dust on in. He already knew it wasn't the
banker's rep, because that kind never forked a horse
or rode so easy.

He recognized the horse before the rider. The little
sorrel of Penny Dickinson herself.

He didn't dismount as she approached, but she
wouldn't just let him set and study. Calling out a
cheery, "Hidy, Cotton!" she dismounted and loos-
ened the cinch of the sorrel like she meant to stay a
spell. Cotton had no choice except to light down to her
elevation and return her greeting.

"Morning, ma'am." He touched his hat.

"Don't be so formal, Cotton." She laughed, her
brown face full of mischief lines. "Just 'cause you're a
man and I'm a woman don't mean we can't be
friendly."

"Yes'm," Cotton said with a little tone of disap-
proval. He thought a lady shouldn't wear pants or ride
a Texas saddle. And yet from whatever anyone said
about her, she could knit and purl as good as anyone.

She kept her red hair tucked up inside a big old
Stetson, and her brown, freckled face looked more like
a sunflower than anything. She was just a little thing,

28

too. Little hands with a worn yellow band still glinting like a warm dream of the past.

"What brings you out this way?" Cotton asked.

"I came out for a cup of coffee," she said. "Brought you a piece of spice cake."

Cotton nodded and went ahead into the camp just in case any of the boys weren't properly dressed. She understood and hung back like a shy filly, until he looked over his shoulder at her and said, "Come on and set down, ma'am."

Kelly, the black cook, poured them mugs of coffee. He was a cook because that's what he did best, same as Wash, the other black man that rode with the herd.

Penny Dickinson smiled and thanked Kelly for the coffee and followed Cotton to sit under the canvas fly, out of the sun.

"You're ready to drive," she said, looking over the austere camp.

"We could be on the trail in five minutes," he said, taking the chunk of spice cake she offered from her bag. "I like to have things set and simple."

"Don't it get some lonesome?" she asked with a little teasing smile.

"A man gets used to it." He was tempted for a moment to ask her to come along and brighten the days for him, but he quickly routed out that idea for the nonsense it was. There'd be enough problems without having to account for a female.

"Don't worry, Cotton." She smiled. "I'm not inviting myself along."

He worked his hands together, wanting to ask her why she'd come, surely not to fetch him a piece of cake, but he reckoned it wouldn't be polite to ask.

"I was in Tres Cruces this morning," she said,

knowing how he would wait and wait before talking, "and the telegraph man had a wire for you."

"That's mighty kind of you."

"Don't be polite," she said, handing over the yellow envelope. "Open it up. I'm as worried as a duck in the desert."

He slit open the envelope with his thumbnail and read the single line twice before reading it again aloud for her.

"Will accept herd in Abilene, at thirty-three dollars per head before July first. Oglethorpe."

"I guess that's what you been wantin' to hear," she said.

"He don't know whether I've got fat, blooded stock or sorefoot sheep."

"Maybe he figures if it's still alive when it gets to Abilene, then it must have some value." She chuckled, wondering at the big man's rock-hard principles. He seemed to her to be like a cloud gathering strength, building up with lightning and storm, a force once started, pure hell to stop.

"Maybe," he said, tapping the paper, "but it don't set right somehow."

"He knows your reputation for square dealing," she said, "same as you know his."

"That's it. I don't know his. Oglethorpe is a mortal human. He can fail."

"Who can't? I mean exceptin' you, Mr. Dunbar."

"Don't mock," he said gravely. "Your herd is important. If I fail, you'll lose your ranch same as I lose mine."

"But I've never known you to fail, and I don't want to tramp on my lower lip neither."

"Sorry to sound so dismal. The land means a lot to

me, and we're stretched out too thin for comfort. My note falls due in August."

"Mine too." She smiled. "But you'll be back before that with enough money to burn a wet mule."

"We'll be off at daybreak," he said, unsmiling, looking out at the horizon.

"I wish you all the luck, Cotton, but you won't be needing it. You'll have a fat herd when you get there, and probably an increase besides."

"No, ma'am," he said, "all I want is what's due, not what can be picked up along the way."

She was standing, her eyes not quite level with his shirt pockets. She was wishing he'd grab her and lift her up and kiss her good-bye, but she wasn't hoping.

He took her hand and held it for a moment, looked her in the eyes and said, "Thank you, Penny, for bringing me the telegram."

"You big damnfool," she said softly, and with a little laugh bounced high and kissed his weathered cheek. His face went scarlet, and she turned quickly and retreated to her horse.

5

Pitch-black and cold as a witch's bosom. Coyote out on his pulpit of bones preachin' at the puny moon. Thick smell of cow and horse sweat. Yawning chuckles and grumbles of rousted-out cowboys smelling the fresh coffee brewing on the grate over a little chip fire.

"Wake snakes, day's abreakin'." Ardie sighed with such misery, the other hands laughed.

Ardie could say "bread and butter" and get a laugh.

"Lordy, Maybelle, where are you now! Ow, wow wow!" Ardie hooted forlornly.

And Yancy Carrol, a box of dynamite packed into the body of a broad-shouldered, small man, asked, "Where'd she be on such a frosty morn?"

"Oh, Maybelle's rompin' in the haymow now, ow ow ow!" Ardie yelled dismally.

"C'mon, Ardie." Kelly smiled. "Have a cup of coffee and put that dream away."

Ardie accepted the mug and swigged down a jolt of

the steaming brew. "Say now, that's good!" He grimaced. "Compared to boilin' tar."

Kelly had baked cornbread and fried sowbelly, hot and ready.

They filled their tin plates and renewed their coffee, while Cotton spelled out their assignments, pairing them up according to their nature as best he could.

"We'll start with Ardie and Deef at the left and right point, Yancy and Chip will take left and right swing, Stacey and Wash left and right flanks, Cass and Joe with the left and right drag. Juan brings up the remuda, and Kelly drives the chuckwagon. I'll be on the scout for water and camp. You rotate by turns every day, and two men stand night guard two hours every night, paired up any way you like."

Stacey looked at the ground and chipped at the dirt with the toe of his boot, but he didn't say anything about being paired up with Wash, the black cowboy.

No one had any better ideas. They knew their partners, knew their best and worst sides, and they were professionals. It wasn't exactly like the army, although Cotton laid it out that way. Anytime a man wanted to quit, all he had to do was say, "Boss, figure out my time."

"We'll rest at noon and rotate for dinner. Now this beef ain't much in the first place, and I'd just as liefer they wasn't too much ganted down time they ramble into Abilene."

The men wolfed their breakfast, listening, but not wasting time palavering. They knew without Cotton telling them that it was make or break for him, and for Penny, for old Deef and Cash on Comanche Creek, and them across the valley, all of 'em honest, hardworking folks who'd got between a rock and a hard place for no fault of their own.

Plates cleaned, mugs empty, they wobbled on their bulldogger heels to a little meadow nearby, where Juan waited with the horses. He would eat with the cook. Each rider knew his own mounts, and even though the horse might not be his property, each horse was treated as his own.

The riders tossed their own loops and after a bit of gentle cussing, had their mounts saddled, bridled, and ready for work. No one pushed ahead or lagged back.

Ardie took his turn cutting out his horse, the greenest one of his string, because he was feeling strong and he knew a stormy, weary day would come when he wouldn't feel up to fighting a bronc that could as well have been gentled and worked into a top cowpony when there was plenty of time to do it.

The big roan had crazy eyes, but his muscles were heavy and he looked as if he could ride up to Kansas and back for a morning's breeze.

Had to fight him down to get the bridle on him, and Juan held him while Ardie cinched down his two-bore rig and climbed him quick as a cat. The others stayed off as the roan tried to swaller his head, but Ardie had a short grip on the reins and held his chin in so's he had to take it the way it was. Then the roan tried throwing his head back and rarin' up with an idea maybe of going on over and rolling over his rider, but Ardie hit him hard with his fist right between the ears, hit him as hard as he could, and he had a hard hit.

At the same time Ardie jabbed him in the flanks with his Mexican spurs, and that was enough to set the roan off on the right direction. Only then did Ardie give a little yahoo. "Kiss me good-bye, Maybelle!"

There was nobody could touch Ardie for funnin', and every soul there, including the inscrutable old Deef, knew it and was glad they had him along.

Cotton had been the first to ride out to the holding grounds where the herd rested. A few steers were up and browsing, a poor collection, but the best they could drag out of the brush.

The purebred Herefords had failed their first test in Texas, but they'd got some of their blood into the southern herds before they died. The short-legged breeds couldn't adapt all that soon to the new land, new feed, new bugs, and they died or aborted and broke the progressive cattlemen that'd dared to try something in the way of improving the breed.

Cotton thought if he made out with his cows, he'd pay the note off the ranch and buy some white-faced mixes, something that could stand the country and fatten on the prairie.

But if the debt couldn't be paid, he'd have to give it all up, the ranch, the graves of his wife and boy, the terrible labor it had taken to cut such a place out of the wilderness; it would all go to the bank, and he would start on west or maybe south, to try something else as honorable.

But in the lavender light of that cool, quiet morning he wasn't thinking in terms of defeat or losing the homeplace, he was thinking about getting the bulls and those mean steers, just lately cut and healed up, moving north.

The telegram and contract were carefully folded into his waterproof wallet.

He spoke to the cattle, "Up now, up now, goin' north now . . ." And awkwardly the misshapen steers hoisted their hind legs and lifted the front and stood around, huddling in headdown confusion. You had to handle them like they was sorefooted and crazy, you had to sing hymns to them at night to keep them steady, you had to waken them with soft baby talk, or they'd bolt back into the scrub and fight you for a week before you could get them back to scratch again. Cotton knew, and the hands he'd hired all knew, the grief of gathering stampeded cattle. They learned the hard way to never say a quick word, strike a sulfur match on a dark night, kill a rattler with a gun, or open a yellow slicker suddenly, even if it meant you was goin' to be soaked all day for goin' slow and easy. Anything was better'n tracking wild cattle.

They grew into the habit of speaking soft and slow amongst themselves, as if the wild cattle had taught them the language.

Cotton stood in his stirrups, looking north, raised his hand high and pointed north. "Move 'em out!"

Ardie pressed behind his bunch and saw old Deef on the right point, easing out his leaders whilst the boys on swing and flank were squeezing the herd to follow and the boys on drag were making sure they lost no stragglers. It would take an hour and be daybreak before the whole herd was moving in its line on trail, but it would be moving steady as two thousand half-tamed, four-footed beasts could move.

It might take a week for them all to get into the rhythm, the routine of walking north sixteen hours a day, but they'd learn it, and after that, all they'd have to worry about would be an infinite variety of natural and human disasters that could happen most anywhere, any time.

In a week they'd be ready to face the Red River, maybe.

Move along, move along, move on, keep amovin', the gentle voices urged.

The striped and spotted cattle with their great sweeping horns on slender heads trudged resentfully up the long trail.

Even with the best days, a rider counted himself lucky to get six hours sleep of a night, because Cotton started early, moved slowly, camped late, and insisted on a double night hawk, though there wasn't an Indian or jay hawker within a couple hundred miles.

Even Ardie was beginning to remark on the monotony, as if he was hoping a rattler would crawl into somebody's bedroll, or a wagonload of sporting girls might be lost along the trail and be needing assistance.

They hadn't seen a ranch house in a week, but from the tracks, and distant dust clouds, they knew there were other herds moving north, too.

Cotton tried to figure every move ahead of time, every bend in the trail, each watering and bedground, and he saw that each horse was rode out but not galled, and he saw that Kelly had plenty of hot food for the men when they came in, and he tried to see that even if they only had a few hours to sleep, it was all theirs to sleep in.

He was always figuring ways of making life smoother and the work a little more pleasant. Like the chuck box on the back of the wagon with the fold-down table, and the cowhide possum belly he had strung under the wagon where the cook could throw in fuel for the night's fire as they moved slowly up the trail to a place they'd never been before.

* * *

Alone, Cotton stopped his pony on a hilltop lookout and regarded the iron-gray clouds to the west and north with pure distaste. He liked water to come in gentle showers, not in the sullen belching cloud bursts that overflowed the creeks and flooded the rivers above all chance of safe crossing.

The expanse of rumbling, tumbling water in front of him was bad enough, but to know that it wouldn't drop so long as those blue-black clouds hung on out there at the headwaters of the Red was a mite discouraging.

You couldn't argue with weather or waste your strength disputing its power. A crazy man could wave the herd on, tell the punchers to put 'em over, and they'd all try and all drown and the weather wouldn't even bat an eye. That was part of bein' boss of a crew that'd do what you asked 'em to do. They'd go ahead, figuring you knew more than they, figuring you was lookin' out for them about as much as the cows and horses, so you had to be extra careful with power like that. He'd say "Ardie, sir, lead your men up that slope and run them there Yankees back to Pennsylvania," and he'd salute you and say "yessir" and go out and lead 'em up as long as there was something to lead, or maybe mercifully it'd get dark and overnight maybe some other general would get the idea that he was sending men up the slope and only their blood was running back.

If the idea of success or goal was to see how much blood you could run down a slope and pool into a ravine, they were doing very well. But if you thought the goal was to outsmart and outwalk and outfight the bluecoats, then maybe you better start smartenin' up, and maybe during the night some poor soul would pass the word to withdraw and you'd slide on back down through the bloodless bodies of the boys who'd gone as far as they ever would.

Times then you wanted that general caught, bound, and shot dead by the troops. But they never shot them, or hung them. They had a way of spreading the guilt around so's even if you knew he was your man and he had given the order, you still couldn't get him. You could not speak to him. You could spit close to his boot when he tramped by, you would give him every chance to call you out, but you couldn't just execute him for being a butcher of his own kind.

The others would say, "Cotton, it ain't that black and white."

They all said Cotton was too righteous, and after a while they wouldn't hardly speak about anything to him for fear he'd crack the whip again. Iron is iron, a knothead is a knothead, and right is right.

After it was over and you studied it awhile and saw they wasn't a chance of a snowball in the hot place of beating the northern money, and that's what it was all about, and you give them four years of your life, you give them wounds and burns and puke and sores, you give them your life's savings, and your wife and child, you give them everything, they knowed all along they was just playing out parts in a play the weather could've wrote. He was sick of it. Next time, old weather, leave me out'n your crazy plays 'cause there's nobody winning anything excepting maybe the northern bankers, and they don't even need it.

Had they just let him alone, he'd never heard of Hood's Brigade, he'd of stayed home and whipped the Comanches and got his spread to working and his children growing up into men, and his little dark-haired wife could be tending her turnips and orphan calves.

"Ah, the blazes!" he said out loud. It seemed that gloomy weather and natural impasses always made him dredge up those old days, even though he knew they had flown away like crows from a bitter harvest. The only thing that made such a grief acceptable at all was that most everyone he knew was suffering, just as bad or worse. Penny Dickinson for one.

But he could never get around to talking to her because he could feel Tom's ghost looking down over his shoulder. How could he hold her in his arms with the warmth of wanting and the ache of years of pure loneliness? It wasn't right. And if it wasn't right, he couldn't go it, no matter how much he might be wishing otherwise.

Funny thing was that most folks figured he had no feelings, that he had icicles for veins. No difference. It was his way. Others had theirs. Happened he could live with himself better for being his own independent man.

He slanted another look at the dark clouds in the northwest, welcome for the grass, but pure misery for his drive because north Texas was a bog this spring already, and you had a hard time keeping your backside dry through the nights.

He turned his pony. Have to make camp and bedgrounds on a higher bench than here. Take three, four days at least before that river would drop.

The herd ahead had made it across the day before just before the rise leaving the land all to him. Maybe it was just as well to have to tail back a ways. Better grass and clearer water. Count your blessings.

He rode for higher ground where he could see the slow line of the herd stretched out a mile. There was no dust, only the red and black and brindly herd, and the eight riders moving along in time with them, and bringing up the rear was the chuckwagon and the remuda off to one side, backed up by Juan.

Sound crew. Couldn't do better. In a week's drive they'd worn off the rough edges, sweated out the whiskey and learned every cow by its middle name.

He sat his horse tall and waved his hat in a slow circle. Left point caught the signal and passed the word along. He was already pulling back while right point was crowding over, turning the herd up to the high ground where they'd be safe from a flash flood and easy to see. His signal was enough. Kelly turned the four-horse team off the track, aiming more to the left, coming directly toward the boss so's he could get in and be set up time the boys had wheeled the herd and come in for supper. Just a week and they were working perfectly. Even the wild cattle were more docile, not losing weight, but just too tired to think up mischief.

They'd have a rest in the wet for three, four days, and sometimes that was harder'n work. Wouldn't hurt, though, just to patch up the rips and mend the mistakes that'd turned up.

Main thing was to keep the herd from stampeding into that swollen river.

Burly, black Kelly sized up his camp in no time, keeping in mind a wind might come blasting off the north, and yet holding onto a piece of level ground so's the boys could be comfortable.

He stopped his wagon where it was going to stay;

fetched out some of the dry wood he'd tossed into the possum belly during the day, had his iron grill set up, fire lighted, and coffeepot on even before he started to unhitch the team.

Cotton was off casting here and there in a wide circle to see if there just might be something he'd overlooked, but it was just the empty prairie land, wet and soaking. He'd picked a good, protected spot, high up enough off the regular trail to still have aplenty grass for two thousand cattle. As he cut back to the herd itself, he eyed each animal, each part, hoof, hock, leg, back, neck, mouth, and eyes, seeing them as pieces going up the trail, and each piece had better be right. One damned critter with the fever could wipe out half a herd right before your eyes. But he'd culled them and he'd watched them, and they were proving out to be sound even if they were still a little scrubby and draggle-tailed. Crazy-colored and savage, still they answered to the name of beef.

To him they were the home ranch safe again, and Penny Dickinson's, old Deef's, Cash's, and the feeble Martin brothers, so's he couldn't care much if they weren't all the same size, shape, and color.

The pungent perfume of burning mesquite hit him as he turned his mount over to Juan and almost automatically took a tin cup off the chuck box and squatted by the fire to pour the brown brew. Back at the box he spooned in raw sugar and eased over amongst the men making up their bedrolls and loosening up their legs.

Stacey sat with his back to a rock, filing on the innards of his revolver, hoping to make it shoot faster than anyone else's.

"Plenty damp, Cotton," Ardie said.

"Too much," Cotton agreed. "Set yourselves for three days of wet."

"Old Red's runnin' full," old Deef said.

"Sure," Cotton replied. "We could maybe swim it even now, exceptin' it's near dark, and by morning I figure she'll be more on the rise."

"Why don't we just get up our guts and keep amovin'?" Stacey asked.

"Too late," Cotton said.

"Wasn't too late for that herd just ahead of us." Stacey laughed and looked around for someone to back him up. The others were carefully minding their own business, a little embarrassed by the kid's applesauce.

Cotton didn't want to humble the boy nor make an enemy of him, if only because of his admiration for Penny, but he had to say something.

"It ain't no joke, Stacey."

Stacey stared at him, his silvery eyes like a feisty rat terrier sizing up a tall coon hound, and said softly, "Well, boss, why don't we take a vote?"

"Maybelle . . ." Ardie tried to take the meanness out of the tense moment, but Cotton held up his hand, keeping him quiet, and said in as reasonable tone as he could muster up, "You're talking to the boss, Stacey. If you don't like it, ride out. That's the only way you can vote."

Stacey looked slowly around the camp, and saw the irritation in the other riders' faces. "Hell, I'm just offering a suggestion. Don't make a damn to me," he muttered, and led his horse over to Juan's remuda.

"Maybelle," Ardie cut into the cold silence, "I wonder if you'd let me under your skirt if'n it starts to rain?"

"You got a clothespin for your nose?" Yancy brought out a laugh from the men.

"Maybelle," Ardie howled, "what does this rannie know about you that I don't?"

Kelly stretched out a tarp fly to cover as much as it would in case the rain came this far east, and the boys were glad to help.

"Ardie, case it gets to lightning"—Cotton smiled—"watch them brutes don't take a notion to run over you."

"I don't reckon they're goin' to mind me." Ardie smiled. "But I'll look after myself."

"I'm not so much worried about you, but we don't want them cattle stampeded north into the river."

"You want 'em goin' south?"

"Better west into higher ground. That way it's easier to roll 'em back down next day," Cotton said, poker-faced.

"Maybelle, wake up, you're dreamin' again." Ardie rolled his eyes up.

"Hello the camp!" came a call from outside the firelight.

Each man remained quiet, neither for nor against, just quiet.

"Come on in," Cotton said.

It could have been a band of hardcase rustlers or it could have been wandering Chinese, but it was only one man wearing a great buffalo robe, riding an old white mule branded U.S. Meant nothin' much. A leftover from the war.

His rig was a little better. Saddle looked near new, and had some silver conchas worked into the rigging. A short-barrel saddle gun lay in its boot under his right leg, and he himself was nothing to be afraid of. Older, gray-bearded, heavy brows, and a bumped-up nose. Trying to see his eyes under the big brows wasn't so easy.

"Light down, pilgrim, and have some coffee," Cotton said. He kept it neutral and cold. No point in goin' off the deep end just 'cause a stranger drifts by.

"Thankee," the old man said, stepping down off the white mule and moving him out of the firelight, tethering him to the north-pointed wagon tongue, since it wasn't said just yet whether he could stay the night or not.

"My name is Cotton Dunbar and this is the Bar D outfit."

"Proud to meetcha," the old man said, shaking Cotton's hand. "They calls me Tom Deveroo. And I'm traveling from nowhere to nothin'."

Kelly put a tin cup of sugared coffee in the old man's hand and, without waiting for thanks, hustled on with building his supper stew.

"Where'd you cross?" Cotton asked.

"Far up. I'm travelin' more easterly. Come out of Santa Fe about a week back."

"How's it out there?"

"Ain't nothin' left of it. Just a damned town full of people."

"Whatever was it before that?" Ardie asked, smiling.

"It was busy. They was buyin' furs and sellin' guns and whiskey and such," the old man said intensely. "Now all they sell is tortillas and beans. Place is plumb ruint. Females hardly look at a man now. Spoilt by the money."

"Oh, no, Maybelle, say it ain't so!" Ardie groaned.

"It's a fact. Used to be you could ride in there and just give a little trinket and you could find more friends than you could stand, but they's all spoilt now. I just couldn't take it no more."

Cotton, studying the old man from the shadows, saw nothing dangerous or sinister, only an old mountain man that time passed by, yet it was hard to read a man with a full beard and his hat shaded down.

"You might as well have supper," Cotton said. "We won't be crossin' the Red for a few days."

"I thank you kindly, sir," the old man said. "I sure won't bring no harm, and maybe I can be of some use to you."

"Rest easy," Cotton said.

"Yessir." Tom Deveroo smiled, a snaggle tooth sticking out like a root from a windfall cottonwood. "I been from here to the Green River, where the four winds meet, and never met kinder folks."

"Come get it," Kelly yelled. "I think she'll swaller."

The hungry cowpunchers moved up quickly with their tin plates ready and passed by the big iron dutch oven in the coals simmering with beef chunks and potatoes and onions. They wasted no time talking, and when they had their fill, they leaned back and rolled cigarettes and studied the ground.

"Reminds me of a time up at the Green River when I was just a button," the old-timer said lazily, fetching out a clay pipe and stuffing it with rough-cut leaf. "We was coming in from the summer catch, had beaver skins baled up like ricks of salt cod, and we'd made up the packs for the mules as good as we ever could, using ever' piece of rawhide in camp. Had eight mules carryin' a thousand beaver pelt worth a heap, I promise you. And being as I was the button, course I kept my mouth shut most times, but I did venture to say them mules was carryin' a breakback load. But them others, old Bridger and Kentuck, the old-time liver eaters, they sort of snorted like old bulls, and I shut up again, like I should. The weather was comin' off the Wind mountains. Could see that gray line comin' over full of ice, and we was in a hurry just like you all, 'count of we'd stayed just a day or two extry to drink some whiskey and lie up with the squaws. But then we settled down to make a run for cover, never thinkin' we'd worked a year for what them mules had on their backs.

"Make a long story short, we come to the Yellowstone, she was runnin' a gorge full. Oh mercy, she was rumblin' and white frothin', and I said to myself, Tom Deveroo, you better look sharp, and I told my little brother Oliver, you stick close, we goin' to get driftwood in our ears, and I said, 'Mr. Kentuck, don't it seem kindly high?'

"And he sang out to them other old alligator he-wolves, sang out, 'Say, boys, don't she seem a leetle high?' laughin' like a loony buck squirrel in a nut farm, and they was all bluff and swagger, you know. Good Christ, they'd gone through that wilderness year in and year out, had become like animals that lived there, y'know, but still holdin' the human weakness of pride, and so they was bound to show me and my brother how the alligator grizzlies did it, an' old Kaintuck, he dallied the lead rope of them mules to his horn and slapped his spurs to his horse and in they went. The others was beatin' on them mules, makin' 'em go, and down into that white water they went, and you never seen any face so surprised as old Kaintuck McGiffin's when his horse was pulled out from under him by a line of floatin' mules bobbin' down the rapids like corks on account of them packs of light, dry pelts. 'Course when they soaked up, they all sank along with Kaintuck and Red Johnson and another damnfool. Me'n my brother and a couple others made camp and waited for the river to drop, and she didn't drop and the snow was whirlin' in on us, and that's when old Jim Bridger said, 'Boys, we better find a cave and kill a bear 'cause we'll never see St. Louis this winter.'"

He stopped, puffed his pipe thoughtfully and stared at the dying fire as if remembering that day when a year's dangerous work was lost in the turbulent river.

"I reckon you made it," Ardie drawled.

"Oh, yes, me and Oliver walked it through deep snow, but we made it. Came into St. Louis dead broke, of course. Nobody cares that you had a thousand beaver skins, point is, you ain't got nothin' now. Our feet was bleedin', but nobody could spare us boots. That's when Oliver taken up the gun."

"Oliver Deveroo?" Cotton asked plainly.

"Guess I'm the only one who'll stand up for him and explain his wicked ways."

"Ain't no explainin' what he did to that Compson girl," Cotton said dryly.

At the mention of Oliver Deveroo the men went quiet, as if their breathing might in some way condone that man's rape and butchery of a pretty little farm girl.

"Don't 'spose it'd do any good to say that Oliver

wasn't within a hundred miles of Compson's when that girl was kilt," the old man said wearily. "Nobody's heard Oliver's side of it. And he can't come out in the open to explain for fear of lynchin'."

"Keep the guards on two at a time," Cotton said, a note of disgust in his tone. "I'm turnin' in."

6

The old man had his pipe stuck into his great bushy beard so's you couldn't see much of him excepting his hawk beak and smoke curling out of his whiskers. He was bowed over watching the coals, kind of sad, like he could remember other campfires and a lot of fine old yarns. Made a mournful picture, and most of the boys that had a heart felt bad about it.

Come daybreak he was gone. Him and the best horse in Ardie's string, along with all the knickknacks and coins the boys had left in their warbags. He was a crafty old gent. Could see in the dark like a coon. Finger through a man's goods silent as a snake and pick out the valuables and leave the rest, never making a sound, and then knocking Juan over the head with a six-shooter so's he could take his time picking through the remuda, and riding out so fast nobody'd ever think it sensible to try catching him.

Cotton found Juan holding his head and muttering, *"Cabrón, pinche cabrón . . ."*

Yancy came up saying the gold watch his daddy'd give him was gone, and Joe Benns and Chip had lost money, and even Kelly's gold watch fob with the glass diamond was gone.

"He eat our vittles and set by our fire and he stole from us," old Deef said.

"Probably ought to count our blessings. Way I was sleeping, he could have cut my throat and I'd never knowed it," Ardie said.

"I thought there was something skewball about that old polecat." Young Stacey nodded wisely.

"He might just have his brother Ollie out there with him," Joe Benns said.

"Me and Ardie, Deef and Yancy, can run him down and hang him," Cotton said. "Cass, you take charge, rotate the riders and keep the herd together."

"Why can't I go?" Stacey's face was flushed with anger.

"I want you here," Cotton replied quietly.

"You just keep treating me like a pesky kid and you're goin' to get a surprise you won't like," Stacey blazed, his pale eyes aglow with anger.

"Ease off, trooper," Cotton replied mildly. "Your turn will come."

There was a tick-tock of a moment when Cotton feared the boy would lose control and come against him, but it wasn't but a few seconds before Stacey spit and turned away and the boys were saddling up their strongest broncs.

In one of his rare serious moments, Ardie rode alongside Cotton, warning, "Goin' to have to curb that young stud before he does something crazy."

"Give him a little time to grow up," Cotton said. "He'll learn."

"I'd as soon watch a baby rattlesnake grow up in my bedroll," Ardie said, hoping Cotton would remember.

Cotton took the lead, following trail, looking out for tricks because the old man had learned them all. Sure enough, right off he'd rode into some sandstone that hardly showed a mark, so's you got the feeling he might have even done the same thing before to some other herd that had camped along the Red.

Cotton decided he was laying up in the hills above the Red, picking off an outfit once in a while, not killing or taking so much he'd cause a great manhunt.

"We need to see the way that old coon's mind worked," Cotton said. "I'd guess he'll make a false trail northwest or northeast. And only way we goin' to dog him down is cut his true track before he dens."

Ardie nodded. "I don't like a man steals my horse and fingers through my tote sack. He come into camp from the west, remember, so he's aimin' east."

"That'd put him above the river," Yancy said. "He'd have no way out."

"He can fish and trap. Easier living there like an old wolf than up in the rocks with lizards and centipedes."

"I'm bettin' with you, Ardie," Cotton said. "He must have started his loop about here. Say we head direct for the river. Must be twenty miles, but I think we'll cut his trail."

"We better," Ardie said, thinking about a gold wedding ring he'd been carrying for some time for some purpose, and it was no longer in his warbag. "Maybelle goin' to be throwing rocks at me, I lose her ring."

"Stealing a horse's bad enough, but fingerin'

through a man's goods, they's something bad wrong with it," Yancy agreed.

"Might be his little brother Ollie's in the timber with a long rifle," Cotton said. "Best figure on it."

"I ain't caring about his brother," Deef said, thinking how in twenty years he'd saved up two hundred dollars in double eagles, and now it was in old Deveroo's pocket.

Riding eastward toward the distant river, they could see the tops of tall trees growing on its banks. Plenty cover for any man wanting to hide himself.

No one talked. They coursed across the easy land marked with gentle swales so it wasn't near as hard riding as in the brush or rocks.

The ground being so damp, they could see no dust from the old man's horse, they could only see the big river and its forested sides. Old Deef was shaking his head, thinking they'd never flush the old muskrat out of that much of a timber break, but Cotton held straight on east, thinking the herd was only half guarded and maybe the old man was drag bait to toll out the top riders while Ollie and a couple more gunslingers could take herd and all and drive it north into the Nations.

These thoughts and more crossed Cotton's mind as his horse kept its steady pace. Putting himself in the old man's mind, he could see how they'd be fearful of leaving the big herd half manned. He'd guess that mentioning Ollie would put the fear of ambush into every mother's son of them, and they'd talk a lot and do nothing, or if they did something, it'd only be half-hearted. But he didn't reckon on Cotton putting right and wrong over anything else, a mighty big mistake.

Was no smoke in sight. No sign of a human living anywhere. Just bucked-down timber, best hiding place in Texas probably.

But as they coursed four abreast over a clean wash, they saw the tracks of a long-legged horse heading north.

In a second they pulled up and circled back to the tracks.

"My Blue Boy," Ardie said. "Set those caulks myself on account he lays his flat feet down so slippery like he's always slewing, even in green grass."

"Not more than an hour old," Cotton said.

"Oh, he's been having a good time making loops for us to foller on hard rock." Ardie laughed. "He's just tickled pink the way he's thinking we're running through his changes. Only he don't know we've cut off about twenty miles of his tail."

"He ain't hiding nothing now," Yancy growled, like an old Airedale that's got his scent clear and hot.

"Maybe he means it to be that way. Maybe not," Cotton said.

"You mean he could be leading us right on top of little brother Ollie?" Ardie asked.

"Possible."

"We spread out," Cotton said. "I'll take the track and you all get a half a mile either side. He can only get one of us."

"Maybe we could take turns," Ardie said.

"No time." Cotton was slapping the spurs to his big black and making it clear he was ramrodding it and nobody else was going to take his chances for him.

They spread out on right and left, where no one rifleman could bushwhack them all.

Cotton could visualize the old man flogging the

tired roan along, tired as he was himself. He'd been up all the night waiting for the hands to sleep, then sifting slow and easy through their goods, and then the long ride. His horse'd be tireder than theirs because he'd traveled twice as far. Cotton figured they had all the advantages from now on less'n they was a long rifle hid out over yonder.

The river made an oxbow just ahead of them, swinging its loop far east and back again, making up a purse of land in its curve. On the far point a faint gray wisp indicated a tiny campfire.

Ardie brought his mount up to match with Cotton's to point it out without making any noise other than the windy laboring of the horses. Cotton nodded and held tight to the track while Ardie drove direct for the point of land barely smudged skyward.

Yancy and Deef on either flank held on though their mounts were foaming on neck and flank. It wasn't going to be long now. They all understood that. Yet at the last moment before breaking into the timber itself, Cotton pulled up and signaled them in.

"River's higher here than on up at the ford. We got him to ground, best not get scratched digging him out.

"Deef, take the left so's nobody sneaks between you and the river. Yancy, take the right same way. Me and Ardie'll just mosey up the center."

"Wouldn't hardly believe he'd be so dumb," Deef said.

"Me either," Cotton said. "'Course he thinks we're way on south, lost in his changes. Takes some fancy luck to cut that track after he's played the fox."

"Best figure Ollie's in there with him," Ardie said.

They rode quietly, having to sashay around deadfalls and bunched up driftage, but gradually they came together as the point narrowed, until there was no problem seeing each other. Cotton silently dismounted and the others followed his example. Their six-guns ready, hustling in a crouch, they ran as only bow-legged, pigeon-toed cowpunchers can run, toward the camp.

Dossed out under bark and brush shelter lay Tom Deveroo. Horses fretted in a willow woven pen close by, the roan there, too. Pack sack next to the worn-out mountain man's head, his mouth open as he snored, little red lips inside the gray tangle, a yellow snag for teeth.

Cotton saw two saddles humped over a log, raised his hand and waved the men back. Something wrong!

Two saddles and extra horses could only mean another man was close by.

Any doubt went flying when a heavy caliber slug barked the tree next to Ardie's face. "Oh, my dear Maybelle," he whispered, diving to the ground as the others found cover.

Now old Tom would be up and ready.

The first shot had come from a dark, tight thicket of willows off to the left. If they'd gone ahead into camp, the bushwhacker could have knocked them down two at a time.

But now the odds were more even.

"Keep him down," Cotton said, and as they'd learned in the war, Ardie fired into the brushy mass while Cotton leaped forward and zigzagged quickly to a fallen log. Hardly had he bellied down behind it than it clunked and shivered from the impact of heavy rifle fire.

A shot came from the right where old Tom had holed up, forcing Cotton to squirm farther to the left until Yancy peppered the camp with his thirty-thirty saddle gun.

"Yo!" Cotton yelled, and fired off four shots into the thicket while Ardie did a crazy run to the log and dropped alongside.

"Once more and I'm on him," Cotton said, reloading his Colt. "Ready?"

"As ever. Got to watch over there for Tom, remember."

"Deef and Yancy can pin him down long enough."

"Whenever," Ardie said. "Maybelle asked me to come home early for apple pie."

"Now," Cotton snapped, and Ardie blazed away at the bushwhacker's hideout while Cotton leaped to the left then right and made a running dive to the edge of the thicket only a few feet away from the hidden rifleman.

Now it was six-gun territory, the rifle too slow and clumsy in the tangle of branches.

A heavy bullet dropped leaves an inch above Cotton's head. Squirming to the right, using downed timber for cover, he saw a rifle barrel glint, and flatted on the ground as another slug buried itself in the duff beside him. But that glint of metal was enough to set him loose. Knowing precisely where the enemy was made the battle even, and he wasn't fool enough to wait for another shot. Leaping to his feet he ran hard on a diagonal, flanking the big windfall where the rifleman hid.

"Now!" he yelled as he dived behind a hummock of mossy earth and Ardie made his run to the left, getting behind the man.

They had him in between. He couldn't shoot both ways at the same time.

"Come slow," Cotton yelled, and let go three random shots to keep the man down.

Cotton could almost see the human form in the shadows. From yonder came Ardie's covering fire, and Cotton made another run straight ahead to the bole of an old sycamore.

The rifleman couldn't stand the pressure of the two men coming at him from two sides, and fired a volley as he ran to the rear, trying to circle toward the horses.

For a second he was in the open, obscured only by the shadowed pattern of aspen leaves, and Cotton, with pure trained instinct, fired without aiming or thinking, and the man screamed and fell.

"Hold off, he's down," Cotton yelled to Ardie.

Cotton heard the wretching and the clogged coughing as the man kneeled on the earth, trying to throw up the blood that was filling his chest.

Lung shot, Cotton thought, and yelled, "Give him another couple minutes, don't rush him."

He heard the man whimper and heave dryly, and Cotton came forward on hands and knees until he was close enough to see the man hunkered over a mossy log, the rifle loose on the ground.

Quickly he tossed the thirty-forty to one side and saw Ollie Deveroo kicking his life out, his vulturelike features and long, lank, greasy hair puddled in his own blood and vomit. The back of his vest was blown out and swimming with bright blood. His lean body twitched spasmodically.

He fixed his eyes on Cotton and tried to speak but his throat was full and overflowing. His lips tried to make a word that Cotton thought was "please," but he was never sure because the eyes burned out, the jaw dropped, and the dead body writhed like a fresh-killed rattlesnake.

Ardie sighed. "I'm sure glad Maybelle never got a look at that."

"Especially if he was alive and had his Arkansas toothpick at her throat," Cotton said, and turned away. "C'mon, we still got to catch a horse thief."

Yancy and Deef had the camp pinned down as Cotton and Ardie worked their way through the timber to the left until they could see the bark and brush shack.

"Tom," Cotton called, "come on out. It's all over for you."

"Ollie?" Tom's voice quavered.

"Ollie's spread-eagled on a bed of rosy coals right now begging for mercy," Cotton called. "Come on out before you die gutshot."

"What do you aim to do with me, boys?" The old man's voice was brimming with self-pity and weakness.

"What do you expect," Ardie yelled, "for stealing my good horse?"

"I'm real sorry about that, boys." Tom's voice quavered, seeking mercy. "Ollie put me up to it. He'da killed me if I didn't do it."

"I'm going to count three, and if you aren't out of that hole by then, you're going to be some sorry."

"I'm coming out, boys, just don't hurt an old man." Tom Deveroo's voice sounded totally abject and miserable. "I been sick."

"Watch that old fox, Ardie," Cotton murmured. "Keep him covered."

Deef and Yancy came forward and joined up with

Cotton and Ardie as the trembling old gray-bearded man shuffled into the open.

"What you aiming to do with this poor sorry body?" Tom Deveroo whined. "This ain't none of my doin'. It was my brother. He had a hold on me. You can have all the trinkets back."

Cotton regarded the shifty eyes that were visible now that the drooping hat brim was gone.

"We just aim to hang you, Tom, for horse thieving. That's the rule," Cotton said. "Anything else you say is just wasted lies."

"Who give you the right to punish an old, helpless, innocent man?"

"Right is still different than wrong, and you been wrong ever since you was whelped," Cotton said. "I hate to think of all the misery you Deveroo brothers have caused."

"I'm too old to hang. I'm plumb helpless now. If you just leave me be, I'll probably starve to death, but I surely can't harm no one."

"Take off that buffalo coat, Tom," Cotton said.

"You still aim to hang me?" The old man started to unbutton the great coat.

As the heavy coat divided, Deveroo's right hand slipped inside, and in an instant brought out a sawed-off double-barrel greener.

Ardie shot him so fast he could pull only one trigger, the buckshot blowing off his foot and the bottom of his right leg. Suddenly he was dead and toppling off to the side.

Deef studied the still form and said, "Heart shot."

"Wasn't any sense in anything else, was they?" Ardie asked.

"Ruined a prime buffalo robe," Deef said.

They searched through the camp and came up with a tote sack full of gold watches and fobs and money and ladies' jewelry, and they felt no remorse for exterminating the vultures that'd been gouging out the treasure of good folks working their hard way north. Like Cotton said, right is right.

They hazed the stolen horses ahead of them, and none looked back. There was nothing there to see except the convulsed corpses of bullet-shattered men, and just beyond, the surging currents of the flooded Red.

—————————————————— 7 ———

The way ahead was clear because the rampaging river had held them back from the pace of other herds ahead, and Cotton was pleased that the sun and rain had brought back the trampled and grazed-over grass to new rich growth so that his own ribby critters were filling out from the unaccustomed rich feed.

"Them beeves goin' to look slick as tallow, come shippin' time," Ardie commented, riding the point alongside the boss.

"Time'll come folks'll see how fast our cactus-fed longhorns put on the fat from the prairie. We'll be sellin' to folks from here to Dakota. They'll double their money in one year just grazin'."

"You thinkin' on it?" Ardie asked.

"I'm settled, but it's 'bout time you was thinking of something besides a bunkhouse."

"I known a few good women, but I don't reckon they're the sort you're talkin' about."

"I'm talkin' about a schoolmarm or a rancher's

daughter, somebody can carry a share of the load. Them saloon girls you blow your pay on, they can't do anything except giggle."

"And wiggle." Ardie laughed.

"And wiggle," Cotton conceded grimly.

"'Course, you ain't so old you can't start all over, too. Plenty of men have done the same thing."

"I know," Cotton said heavily. "I think about it, but somehow my mind isn't ready just yet. When I think of a good woman I think of my wife first and somebody else second. Someday . . . maybe . . ."

"It's not like you," Ardie said, "to wait for something to happen. Why not just take the old brown bull by the horns and rattle his hocks?"

"Right now all I want is get this herd into Abilene, pick up the money and get back home."

Looking back over the mile-long ribbon of slow-moving cattle, Cotton felt a sense of pride, but thinking of the long miles ahead, the rivers to cross, the badlands, the outlaws, he quickly put the surge of optimism down. It wouldn't pay to start counting the chicks just yet.

For while the cows were getting fat and sleek, the drovers were becoming lean and dark from the widening days, their tempers a bit shorter, their movements toward day's end a little slower.

Their mounts had worked the kinks out, and there were no saddle sores, because Cotton insisted they ride at least three different horses a day.

But there was never one day like the day before or one night the same as any other night. You mix up wild cattle, weather, and new country, and nothing is going to be the same.

You started every day thinking it would be a catastrophe of some kind. Some mornings you didn't even get time to think.

"I'm goin' to pick a bedground," Cotton said, glancing at the sun and turning off even as Ardie habitually crowded up on a big yellow bull who was always wanting to bear off to the west.

Ardie wondered if they were traveling south, would the bull always ease off to the east? Maybe he was sorefooted on one side, or blind in one eye, always wanting to go left.

"Just like me, grulla John," he said to the yellow bull, slapping him on the left shoulder with his quirt. "I'm goin' a way I don't even know why."

Cotton rode ahead. When they bedded down in a couple hours, they'd want clear water and deep grass. A big table would be better than a slope cut up with sharp-sided gulches and a passel of buffalo wallers, but that's all there was. Miles of it. The grass not bad with water in the coulees, but it meant a split-up herd, and it meant the night riders would need to be alert to make their rounds through the horse deep coulees. Cotton didn't like it. He rode west and found it not much better. He rode east and found it worse.

Weather was changing. A little blue-gray to the south was coming up. But it wasn't the cloud so much as the smell of the air—sultry, kind of smoky, like after the lightning strikes close by.

He couldn't pick ground any better'n this, and he sure couldn't fool with the weather; he could only get his herd in the right place and his drovers on their best horses.

Cotton gave the arm signal, saw Ardie's hand raise in acknowledgment. Lifting out his saddle gun, Cotton rode on upland, hoping to find a deer for the crew. A man could get plumb weary and lose his appetite on tough beef every day, but there was nothing about except an old badger digging out a den a horse could break a leg in.

The boys had the herd milling slowly as darkness fell. The scent of electricity still hung in the air, and the humidity drew out what little juice the riders had left in their wiry bodies, soaked their shirts and made their butts raw from the salt working against the saddle, but they kept with the herd till the leaders settled and the main body paunched down to chew their cuds and rest their legs.

"That new grass makes them fractious," Cass Curry said to Ardie. "If 'twas me, I'd drive 'em harder so they'd want to rest when they got the chance."

"Boss wants to slick 'em up for the buyer," Ardie said.

"Sure, maybe we get a dollar a hundred extra for good looks, but we might lose two dollars a hundred in piled-up runaways."

"I reckon he figures it's our job to see they ain't any runaways."

"You seen them coulees, them cutbanks?"

"One or two little furrows." Ardie grinned.

Cass laughed at the deadpan understatement. "Furrow! I just hope your pony can jump them furrows!"

Yancy and Chip were left to guard the herd. You could hear them singing some kind of bastardized hymn in the distance as their ponies picked their way around the herd.

Kelly had a big pot of beans, fried beef, and salt raised bread. They filled their plates, making rude jocular comments on the tough beef and routine beans. When Cotton rode in through the gloom, Juan took his horse.

"Saddle me the pinto, will you, Juan?" Cotton asked. "And fetch him back here to the wagon. I might just need him in a hurry tonight."

Turning to the men hunkered around the fire, he suggested mildly, "Maybe everybody better keep a good night horse ready and close by before you bed down."

"See some wolf sign out there?" Deef asked.

"No, nothin'. No venison, nor wolf. Just badger holes. But it's something in the air got my back hair up. No point in wishing it away. Best be safe than sorry."

"We can double the guards," Joe Benns offered.

"Not yet, anyways. It's something I don't put my finger on, and it's been a long day already."

"I was feelin' something myself besides the humidity," Cass said. "Smelt like flint struck on iron."

Wash nodded. He'd smelt it too, but they didn't have a name for it, and it was invisible.

The chuckwagon and camp were located well above the cattle's bedground and separated by the fork of a watercut coulee. Cotton didn't eat, he walked outside the firelight trying to discover what was bothering his sixth sense. The remuda was safe in another draw, unless there were Injuns about, but it was the wrong time and place for them. Wasn't animals. Could be rustlers setting up to take a chunk of the herd, but that was just an everyday worry he lived with. Weather was clabbering up, but it wouldn't rain at least tonight. Maybe it was just the sultry heat that was sweating out the dry cowboys and their horses and irritating the beeves.

For sure there'd be no sleep for the boss. He'd be drifting around easy, his six-gun loose. But mostly he'd be wary, sniffing the heavy air like a wolf, waiting it out till daybreak.

Best not do any wild gunplay, because any shot, any pop of slicker or saddle blanket, would send the nervous herd out the chute and halfway back to San Antone. You just had to wait it out, ride softly, sing softly.

The campfire dwindled, fed only by buffalo chips and a few cottonwood limbs Kelly'd picked up along the old washes. Country was getting drier, with only a scattering of timber in the river bottoms.

Cotton hunkered by the fire tossing in a bit of grass or twig to keep it going and the coffee warm. He was alone; the riders had all taken their boots off and crawled into their soogans. Kelly was in his blankets under the wagon, having left the coffeepot full and the dough for hoecakes rising while he caught a few hours sleep.

The stars overhead didn't seem to come through crystal sharp like they normally did, they were wavering and changing colors in between some murk or haze, hard to say what it was. Call it humidity, call it anything, Cotton reflected, but don't call it trouble.

His big hands were wrapped around a mug of black coffee. His ears were tuned to the sounds of the night, the snores and groans of sore-boned cowboys, the old coyote out yonder mocking his troubles, and the little prairie owl giving his curly whoo-it whoo-it and soaring by like a shadow. Some frogs in the water holes were baying like bulls, and once in a while a horse'd cough and a cow would take a deep breath of the heavy air.

Little bells tinkled from Cotton's spurs as he shifted his weight, listening, feeling, soaking it in so much he was a piece of the darkness grafted in it so well you wouldn't know where the night joined into him.

Yancy rode in about midnight. You could hear the thudding of his horse's hooves coming through the ground before hearing them through the air. The vibration awakened the relief couple, Ardie and Wash —so used to it, they were slipping into their boots before the actual rider appeared to give them word.

"Be right there," Ardie said.

"Me, too," Wash said.

Yancy rode on to the remuda, stripped his rig and tossed it onto a Roman-nosed chestnut Juan had staked out on a picket line for him.

Time he was back to the fire, Ardie and Wash were drinking their sugared coffee and sniffing the swampy air.

"Smells funny, don't it?" Wash said. "Smells like a Louisiana swamp."

"That's what makes it strange. Louisiana on the Panhandle," Ardie said softly. "Now listen, Wash, I'm going to keep singing on my rounds steady on, and you better, too. If they run, we'll know where the other is and can turn 'em together instead of against each other."

"Sure thing," Wash said. "I'll be warbling like a bird wishing for wings if them steers get a motion to light out."

Cotton said nothing, didn't seem to pay any attention. He didn't need to tell them anything they didn't know or wouldn't do. But as they left the firelight, he said, "You might hear me singing out there, too. If there's a choice, I'd liefer head 'em uphill as down."

"We'll see," Ardie said, cinching down the bright sorrel horse, the brightest colored horse in his string. He wanted them steers to see him.

Wash rode a splotchy-paint Injun pony, white and red.

They loped easily to the bedgrounds, Wash taking Yancy's spot on the east, Ardie going on around easy and softly to the west, where he could hear Chip's cracked tenor warbling a lot of nonsense to the resting herd.

Coming up on him, Ardie sang a few words to make himself known. Chip waited a minute to pass on whatever he knew. "It ain't much you can really put your lassrope to," he muttered to Ardie, drifting alongside, "it's just they ain't sleepin'. They'll lay down awhile, and then one of 'em'll snort and get up and wander around awhile like he has a tick in his ear or something. They ain't scared, but they ain't sleepin' neither."

"You better try some of that sleeping stuff. There's not too much of it around here anymore," Ardie said.

Chip faded off, the regular beat of his horse skying off toward camp, and Ardie commenced humming a tune as he heard Wash far across the herd tone out some of the prettiest music in the world.

Ordinarily Ardie would be still just so he could hear Wash's voice rising and falling through the night with its patterned rhythms and natural composition all just borned to the black rider, but tonight he had to sing his own tune too, just to soothe the weather.

Hear me yonder, hear me down below,
Hear me yonder, hear me down below,
Hear me yonder, hear me down below,
Got more steers to handle
Than a goddamn rodeo . . .

It was just a way of making up words to a tune as old
as people, and the words were always changing. It gave
a man something to think on as he rode through the
darkness around the mass of half-tamed brutes.

Across yonder Wash was singing:

Looo—eeeezz—iaaannnaaa low lands,
Lowlands, l-o-w-l-a-n-d-s, l-o-w . . .
Loooo—eeezzz—iannaaa, low—ooo—oow—

Later on when he warmed up to it, he'd put some
words in it, words as smooth and long as Louisiana
low.

But even as he sang, another part of Ardie's mind
was thinking he'd like to set up the stars in pictures
the way they did in olden times, but using his way,
they'd be pictures of the cowboy's life. Instead of
Orion's constellation—his bow, belt, and sword—
it'd be the strawberry roan throwing Bill Wolverton in
Jackson Square in New Orleans, a legendary battle
between man and horse: the horse winning, at least
that once. The brightest star in the constellation was
the roan's hot flashing eye as he soared up for his final
throw.

And that one they called the Plough. That'd be the
Texas Longhorn. Hell, you could see him picked out
in the stars like conchas on a señorita's vest. You could
see those long, sweeping horns looking like they never

belonged on a prairie beast, and the other stars pointing out the outline of a huge longhorn in the murky, shimmering sky.

Looking at the sky above the lumpy mass of cattle, some of them with their heads up nervously, Ardie saw balls of yellow light suddenly, magically, appear like stars on their upraised horns!

He wouldn't have believed his eyes if he hadn't seen it happen before and heard it called all kinds of things like Swamp Fire, Fox Fire, St. Elmo's Fire. Out here, whatever you called it, it was bad. The steers saw the balls of golden light beaded down their horns and over the upthrust and frightened ears, a ball on each muzzle, and beading on down their briskets as they arose in one lunging body. Even the big sorrel had beads of yellow light spaced like golden bells along the reins and on top of his ears, and call it what it was, it was the worst thing could ever happen.

Popping of horns made it double as they tangled in the first wild-eyed rush. Now it was all noise of horns and hooves. They were following after the leaders on the first rush, almost as if they had it planned how to make the break out. From far across uphill came the stronger voice of Wash singing out any way he could as he tried to work back, knowing the orders were to turn 'em uphill, and he had to skedaddle back out of the way without getting killed and at the same time hope Ardie could come up on the off side of the leaders and turn 'em up the slope.

Some question whether a man could or couldn't even catch up with the leaders at first, let alone ride in close and crowd 'em over. A big job for a lone cowboy and his pony, but Ardie was making a hell of a lot of noise, whether it was singing or calling on Maybelle for help, and doing his best to crowd his pony in against the running steers.

Was no point in shooting anything, just spook 'em out all the more. The point was to gentle them and put them to milling. Ardie knew how Wash was making the long hard circle clear around at a breakneck gallop to side him, and then he heard, coming up right ahead of him, the strong voice of Cotton, bellering an off-key croon and sticking his own mount into the leaders, making them bend uphill, and between the two of them they were doing pretty fair, and along came Wash to make it three pushing in at the point, making the running snake turn in against his tail, making him run uphill and wear him out before he got himself scattered and stacked up in the coulees.

Horse and man were one, connected through the knee grip of the man and the balance of his body. Wasn't time for thinking, only thing was to keep whipping on their heads and stay off their horns. Wasn't all that easy on hidden ground and murky stars, and the yellow globes glowing on their horns didn't give out any light to see by.

Ardie hardly felt the horn slice through his boot and bash the flank of his pony. The sorrel didn't protest or flinch, he just kept at it right along with his other half telling how to go with the pressure of the knees.

Off yonder Ardie could hear riders joining up, bending the snake into circling on itself, and he was trying to keep an eye on the boss who was bearing hard in on a big black bull, smacking him across the nose with his quirt and cussing a blue streak. About that time he saw the boss disappear along with the horn-lighted black bull, just disappear into nothing, and Ardie swerved hard left, knowing there was something ahead he didn't need. Cutting a little circle, he let Wash go on the right while he rode slower, looking for where the boss and the black bull had disappeared. Finding the sharp cutbank, he sidled and slid down it sideways, the sorrel spooked but still willing. At the bottom of the gulch, below the thunder of the herd, he saw the thrashing bodies of bull, horse, and man, tangled in leather and twine.

Ardie was off his horse in a second, put his revolver beneath the bull's horns and fired so that he would die without a kick or wild motion, just die without a quiver.

That left the terrified horse, and Ardie could see his broken foreleg, its raw white stump sticking out of the hide, the rest flopping. Another shot and the horse was as still as the earth, its cries of pain extinguished. That left the man who was making no motion nor any sound of pain.

"Easy, Captain, easy now," Ardie said to the still form. "What's the matter? Knock the wind out'n your brisket? Shoot, you'll be first one at the bean pot come morning, I betcha, or Maybelle goin' to be disappointed." And as he chided and teased and cajoled the still form of the man, Ardie carefully untangled the living from the dead. They'd come over the bank in a ball, the horse ripped by a horn, the bull broke his lower back, and the man, what about the man caught in the middle?

Blood across his face. Leg caught in the stirrup next the bull's butt. "Steady on, Captain, you goin' to be jumpy as popcorn in a skillet right soon. Give you a little drink of twenty rod and you'll be taking the hide off the first puncher that cracks a smile . . ."

Ardie by then had the big man dragged free of the

animals, and he labored over the battered form, which he discovered was still breathing.

"Well, hell, if you're still pumpin' wind, Captain, they sure ain't killed you," Ardie said with great relief. Life was life. Without it you didn't have much to go on.

He gathered up some dry grass to make a marker fire, adding on bits of anything that'd burn, hollering, building up his blaze, and finally, still keeping his voice loud, feeling the unconscious form for broken bones. Blood came from a nasty cut across the forehead. Lots of blood, but wasn't nothing to hurt a Texican, and the rest of him seemed in one piece, except you couldn't tell if he might have knocked his spleen loose on the saddle horn as he fell. Chances were a man as muscled as the Captain would've broke the horn off instead of his belly, and it added up to a break in the lower end of his right leg. Nothing to that. Ardie set about straightening the leg out as best he could.

Best to do it while the boss was unconscious. Had to stick his foot into the boss's crotch to get leverage enough to bring the bone back and out and true.

In a short time Kelly rode a mule in, naturally carrying splints made of spruce slats and an old sheet they could rip into long lengths of bandage.

"He goin' be all right?" Kelly asked as they worked in the faint, flickering light.

"I expect. How's the herd?"

"They up yonder. Still movin', but the boys is with 'em."

"Can you bring the wagon anywhere close by? I just don't rightly remember where we are and the way things was awhirling up above."

"I can come pretty close."

"Go ahead and fetch up."

Kelly left on a run, and Ardie stripped the boss's tack off the dead horse before it started to swell. Ardie took the hot horse blanket and laid it over the still form with its white bandaged leg, and wrapped a couple yards of bandage around Cotton's head just in case of a fracture.

The rumble of the milling herd lessened and the distant yipping of the cowboys lost its intensity. Suddenly Ardie felt bone tired. He tossed a few strands of grass on his fire and reflected if Cotton hadn't taken the point from him, it'd been him laying here in a deep coulee with a dead horse.

"Wish't I had a drink of whiskey, Captain," Ardie said. "One for you and two for me. I think I'm feelin' some more misery than you right now.

"'Course, soon as you open your big blue eyes you're goin' to be feeling something more'n me—that is, if you are capable of any feeling at all ever. Sometimes I wonder if you aren't just all bone and gristle, don't feel nothin' excepting maybe day and night . . ."

"How's the herd?" the still form asked, eyes closed.

"Making a mill higher up," Ardie said, not surprised.

"Reckon they need you now?"

"No. Sounds like it's all over. Them cows is plumb wore off to the knees by now."

"Fox Fire," Cotton said, still not opening his eyes, nor betraying any sense of pain.

"Sure enough. Got to remember when I smell brimstone on a sultry night to go climb the nearest tree." Ardie grinned.

"Ready," Kelly called as he scrambled down the bank. "They's a buffalo trail a little farther down. Best we carry him thataway."

"All set, boss?" Ardie asked.

"Whenever you say."

"It's your right leg. Broke below the knee. Put your weight onto me and Kelly's shoulders, and we'll traipse right on back to camp."

"Horse?"

"Dead. So's the bull."

Cotton didn't reply. He stretched out his arms to grab the two men's shoulders, and they carried him down the coulee to where Kelly had found a sloping trail. The wagon was there, the mules staked to a picket.

"Fetch out the rig in the morning and butcher off the quarters and back straps of the bull," Cotton said as he lay down on the wagon bed and closed his eyes again.

Solid bone, Ardie thought. Big, solid, prime bone.

Kelly clucked to his team and turned toward camp, while Ardie hoofed it across the ravine and up the other slope to find his sorrel horse nibbling at the grass, waiting.

"Another day, another dollar," Ardie groaned, twisting up into the saddle, seeing the bars of sun cut up through the dark eastern horizon.

Every day after was a day of impatience for Cotton, waiting to swing his splinted leg over a saddle.

Three weeks later he climbed aboard his steadiest horse and went on the scout alone.

The crew was lean and flinty as tommyhawks. Growing a little crazy from being on the go all the time, it seemed more like a forced march of a brigade up the Shenandoah Valley under old Stonewall.

They saw sign of the lead herds again, same as when they'd had to wait for the Red to drop.

A couple days later Cotton took the splints off and just wrapped the leg in a rag where it was tender. Never said much, just put the skin-shined wooden splints back in the sawbones box.

Once in a while a stranger might stop and visit, and there'd be a reference sometimes to the Deveroos feeding the ants in a windblown shakedown on the river, but there was no talk of vengeance or follow-up justice. None of the crew would say anything unless the stranger seemed to be pushing hard, then he'd likely get his boots spit on and he'd move out.

Across the Washita, across the Canadian, they had only the old Cimarron to worry about, and by the time they reached its banks, the water was down and summer up, and them beeves wanted nothing better than to sport through the belly-deep stream, whilst the boys kept them out of quicksand holes.

Cotton wiped the sweat off the back of his burned neck and stared across the glaring prairie. Abilene was so near, and they were bone tired. The beeves were dropping some of the tallow they'd picked up in the Nations. Even Ardie was finding it hard to dredge up a grin coming out of his blankets.

"Maybelle!" he'd yell. "Bring me a little drink of cold beer, Maybelle!" But there wasn't so much of a laugh to it as it was seeming near to a serious plea.

"Please, honey, punkie pie! Just a little swaller. One eency swaller for your good little boy, Ardie. Ardie who? What you talkin' about, Maybelle, don't you remember me? Good old big-spending Ardie Rousseau, that handsome, kindly-hearted southern gentleman. Ya don't? Been too long, too dry, and too seldom? Maybelle, have a leetle mercy on a poor wandering cowboy . . ." On and on he'd go, arguing with the fanciful buxom dream girl, but each day she became a little harder to get along with.

Their faces burned browner and pinched up over their cheekbones, making tight creases around their mouths and corrugating their raw necks.

Young Stacey kept to himself, putting in his hours, but his thoughts were somewhere else.

Remembering how his mother had fed the family, Kelly had taken to picking wild greens along the way, dandelion, dock, lamb's quarter, sour grass, and boiling them with bacon grease.

"Take your tonic, boys," he'd say, and the crew surprised him by cleaning up the kettle as if it contained a mysterious magic ingredient.

Hard to keep the guards alert during the long night's patrol, but Ardie seemed to have a secret sackful of songs he could reach into when things looked dismal as a belly-up toad.

> Oh, they chaw tobacco thin in Kansas
> They chaw tobacco thin in Kansas
> They chaw tobacco thin
> And they spit it on their chin
> And they lap it up agin . . .
> In Kansas . . .

8

In the three weeks after Cotton broke his leg, they covered 250 miles, none of them easy. Always something. Steers balky, flies bothering, the drag working like hollow-eyed, dust-choked slaves to keep the weak ones moving along on sore feet. Or there'd be a shortage of flour. Or some harebrained Injuns would get the notion they ought to have beef free for nothing. Or as they drove through the Nations, some squatter would fence in a water hole and charge for a drink.

Cotton stood it only once, couldn't help himself, because he didn't know the water had been taken up by a lanky old sodbuster with a double tube ten gauge backed up by his stringy wife and a small herd of young, barefooted ones. Couldn't shoot him in front of the kids. Had to have the water that night. Beat him down to twenty-five dollars, but it wasn't right, and he'd never do it again.

After that, Cotton and Kelly would ride the wagon ahead to the next water, and Cotton sat in the wagon while Kelly would speak to the nesters. Big and black as night, Kelly could roll his eyes like a duck in a thunderstorm. He carried a big forty-five on his leg, but his best argument was the way he could face a man and state his proposition and grind his teeth. With the sound of those ivories gritting and screeching against each other, and those shiny rolling eyes, you didn't feel too much like arguing prices over something wasn't yours in the first place.

At Crystal Springs just inside the Kansas border it looked as if the drive would soon finish rightside up and sunny. Wasn't but a week's travel left, and they'd be in Abilene easy. Could even take it a little slower and let the cattle slicken up some off the curly buffalo grass in seed.

Crystal Springs was an old-time watering stop, old as the prairies, but of course somebody had dabbed a line of pickets around the flowing limestone ledges and flumed the water off. Some other drive ahead had just got fed up with that kind of nonsense, probably just choked up with dirt and cantankerous critters, and they'd pulled posts and flume clear to hell and gone and shot up the shack until the nester quit and rode off and let it be, but there was still that smell of old habitation and violence.

For now, this day, praise be, the water belonged to every man, and Cotton stood in his stirrups, signaling with his hat to the left point, who passed the signal along to the winding line of herd and riders. They'd put the cattle downstream and let them rile it up all they wanted and wet the fever out of their feet, but this springhead would be for the camp, and it'd be kept pure and crystal like it was named.

Not the best place in Kansas to guard the herd,

Cotton realized, because there were sloping gulches and low hills where you could lose five hundred head easy enough if somebody wanted you to lose them, but he was feeling better just knowing he had crossed into a regular state, instead of a territory. Same ground, same terrain, same air, but on one side there was law and order, or was supposed to be, and a man could be excused for thinking his property was safer once it was in the jurisdiction of the State of Kansas.

He felt the weariness and short temper as much as any. His leg ached every time he stepped wrong on it, and he'd slept a lot less than the rest of them in the past six weeks, but that was what a man did. He did what was right, and he didn't whine when he felt whipped and miserable as a poisoned pup. He just set his teeth and kept his eyes open, and moved on.

From his elevation Cotton watched the long line of cattle come to the water, stop, collect, and mass. Crazy patchwork of colors, healthy, fat, and sassy. They were contracted for, they'd be paid for, whatever they were. The old nagging worry of the day the buyer never came to look at the stock but sent a blind telegram instead, drilled into his mind again. A contract was a contract, and it was binding on both parties. It bound Cotton Dunbar to deliver. That's what he was supposed to do, and he would do it.

Kelly had the wagon set up at the springs and his team turned out before the drag had brought up the stragglers.

Gaining daylight every day, they were driving out earlier in the dawn and bedding them later at sunset. It made for an extra four miles a day though it was wearing on the men.

Using cowchips now, Kelly had a smudge going to

cook on and keep some of the skeeters back. The hands drifted in, turning their tired ponies over to Juan and taking a minute to roll up a quirly and smoke it slow whilst camp was settling down and night falling.

Nothing much left for Kelly to cook except beef and beans. Still had a little coffee, cornmeal, and grease, but things were getting mighty simplified for the cook. With a little time he'd go digging prairie turnips.

"Señor Dunbar," Juan said, eyeing the eastern skyline that was already dark to most eyes, *"un hombre."*

Cotton followed the wrangler's view and discerned a big man on a big horse aiming for the camp. A faint glint of gold gleamed on his shirtfront, his horse a buckskin.

"Looks like he owns the county," Stacey said.

"He's sure welcome to it," Ardie said. "I'll give him Maybelle's share for nothin' if he'll just get me back to Texas."

"Lawman," Cotton said.

Each man felt an itch in the back of his neck and a drifting of his hand toward his six-gun.

"We ain't done nothin'," Kelly said.

"Nothin' we can talk about," Ardie said.

"And we're ten to his one." Stacey smiled.

The big buckskin took his time, tossing out his front feet like a softshoe dancer, wasting motion but looking pretty just the same.

"Got him gaited," Ardie said. "When you goin' to gait my bay, Juanito, so's I can join up with a traveling show?"

"Any time you can set his saddle through two jumps." Juan smiled, thinking about that spirited bay horse that would explode almost any second he felt like it, and he felt like it most of the time.

"Howdy. Come on in and light down," Cotton called, his voice like always, not hard or easy, just saying the words without throwing in any flavor.

The big man pulled up at the edge of the camp and ground tied the fancy horse. "Evenin'," he said to the whole group clustered about the smudge and coals, and speaking directly to Cotton, he said, "My name's Tosh, deputy U.S. marshal."

"We're pleased to be in safe territory," Cotton said, "we ain't seen a lawman for many a long day."

"I'd not say it's any safer than the Nations," Tosh answered, taking the mug of coffee Kelly handed him and a plate of beans and beef, "the way folks complain."

"Complain about what?" Cotton asked carefully.

"Rustling. Seems as soon as they get in sight of the law, they start to lose cattle. 'Course they'd not carry any thought of it if they didn't have somebody to complain to. Lose a hundred cows to the Choctaws, they'd just be mad, but that's about all they'd be. Coming into Kansas, they're mad at the law, too. So just let out your bellyache, I'm used to listening." The big man smiled thinly.

"We're pleased to be here, Marshal," Cotton said.

"Not lost any critters?"

"Not to rustlers," Cotton said. "We've eat a few."

"Them ain't the most appealing cows I've ever seen, maybe that's the secret."

"They got four legs," Cotton said, "and they don't jaw a lot."

"I ain't runnin' them down none," the lawman put in quickly. "Likely it's been a tough road."

"Likely," Cotton said dryly.

"I just come to say there's regular rustlers out this way. They like to sneak up at night, pop a blanket and cut a piece of the herd out in the stampede. They run 'em around to the west and sell 'em to the mines in Colorado."

"Good price out there?"

"Hard to say. Depends on the weather. Wintertime they sell high, summer they're not much. Beef ain't worth anything now anywhere."

"What'd you mean?" Cotton asked, a little fear edging his voice.

"Market's dropped out. They say there's something wrong back east. Can't find no cash money."

"'Course we ain't working on tick," Ardie said.

"That's right," Cotton said. "We're contracted."

"Don't make no never mind to me," the lawman said. "My job is to warn folks to look out for them Colorado boys. They know what they're doin', and they ain't afraid to use their guns to do it neither."

"Why don't somebody round 'em up?" Stacey stepped forward.

"There's only me. One man. I'm willing to head up any posse that wants to run them snakes down."

"Let's do it," Stacey put in excitedly.

"We're due in Abilene next week," Cotton said.

Stacey glanced swiftly at Cotton, set his jaw, but said no more.

"Then I'm on my way," the marshal said.

"You can stay the night."

"There's a herd on down the trail about ten miles. They're figuring it's a sleigh ride on into the pens, just like you was before I showed up. That's the kind them Colorado boys like."

84

"Thanks for warning us, Marshal Tosh," Cotton said.

The big lawman, with a certain arrogance, a way of going that set him off from, if not above, the common man, walked to his big buckskin, swung up, and with a little nod was on his way south.

"Didn't even say thankee for the vittles," Kelly grumbled, and tossed the tin plate into a kettle of suds.

"Something though in what he said about rustlers. We aren't inside the pens just yet," Cotton said thoughtfully.

"Shoot, I was set to lay my head between Maybelle's big bosoms through the whole night." Ardie smiled.

"I don't see why we just don't go run them skunks down before they come at us," Stacey muttered aloud.

"I already said. We got a date in Abilene," Cotton said tolerantly.

"We just goin' to set on our butts and give 'em the cows?"

"Easy there, Stace," Cotton said. "We ain't give anything away yet."

Wash rode into camp and without speaking headed for the coffeepot.

"Guess that means it's time to relieve the night-hawks," Ardie said. "Maybelle, saddle up and ride with me tonight, will you?" He shook his head. "She's sleepy. Sure glad I'm the kind that likes to commune with nature."

In a moment he and Yancy were gone into the darkness.

"You know," Cotton said as if he were talking to himself, "if I was goin' to stompede a herd, I'd wait till they were changing the guards and only one man out there. That's when I'd pop my slicker. And I'd do it right on midnight to get five hours of safe darkness. The crew wouldn't even know what they'd lost till they made the round-up next afternoon."

"Trouble is, you don't know which night," old Deef said gloomily.

"Say we figure it was tonight. Say we double the guard about midnight."

"You goin' to have some mighty weary cowpunchers," Joe Benns said.

"We take it a night at a time."

"Better to go out and catch 'em and hang 'em!" Stacey said angrily.

"Maybe we can do both," Cotton responded mildly. "Now let's get some rest."

Edgily, Cotton moved out of the firelight, thinking that someone was watching him, someone out there in the great circle of darkness was counting his cows, his horses, his men, counting his guns and his stock of stubbornness.

Those eyes knew the terrain well, could travel it by night, and they preyed upon the weary, sleep-shot strangers, unavoidably slow in their reactions.

Cotton had the memory of how quick and sharp they'd been down by Austin, compared to their dragged-out, groggy condition now.

"Listen close, Kelly," Cotton murmured from the shadows. "Rig a tarp or something around your fire, and don't show a light."

"Your backbone feelin' them eyes?" Kelly asked.

"Something," Cotton said. "Just don't give any light, and they can't see."

"Yessir," Kelly said, already dragging out a piece of canvas for a screen. "I just hope they ain't hants."

"I'm bound to make a pasear out there," Cotton said, shifting his gun belt forward and easing off into the blackness of the night.

By the wagon, he quickly pulled off his boots and slipped into soft-soled moccasins.

Trying to remember the lay of the land, he realized how fuzzy-minded he'd become himself. The details of the camp were clear enough, but the coulees and the high knolls were confused in his memory.

He forced his mind to take it a picture at a time. If he was going to spy on camp and herd, where'd he be? Thing about Crystal Springs, everybody knew it and used it, so a rustler could come through here once a week and have it all set up his way, knowing the whole game before it was even played. Way to beat him was to do something different, change the scheme and make him the weak one.

'Course, no way of knowing there was anybody out there at all excepting night feeders, coyotes, possums, and such, but Kelly'd felt that presence, the curly feeling up the backbone, and he trusted Kelly's senses as much as his own. Should let Kelly sneak out and fetch the hidden eyeballer in because he could probably do it better, but then again it might be a choice of whether to kill or not. He was on a wage. Cotton didn't figure you asked a man on a wage to kill your snakes for you.

There was only one high place. It stuck out like a limestone snout over the spring and creek, and yet you couldn't get to it except on the roundy-bouty. Man could lay up there and see everything that went on in camp.

How much had the thing seen of him, of Kelly, or maybe heard his orders of the blind around the fire, a dead giveaway something was suspicious? Would the lookout know he was being stalked in the darkness?

One thing at a time. You do each step right, chances are the end'll come out right, too. Cotton moved left instead of right, where it was easier going. Keeping low to the ground and making no sound, he eased far out and met the corner of the limestone cliff breaking off to the level ground. But he went another quarter mile farther out into the darkness, still not knowing what was where, only knowing you did one right thing at a time and maybe it's wasted, but at least it's done right, and now on the backswing coming in from high and far out, he had it better than he expected. He'd outflanked it.

He was above it and behind it.

If it was there at all.

Sure didn't want to fire a shot. Same as poppin' a slicker on the herd. They'd go pronto and scatter in these chopped-up brakes.

The big bowie was in his belt sheath. It would be better than the Colt with those gun-shy mavericks in hearing range.

Moving across the slight slope, no brush, no trees, but no moon yet either.

No smell of tobacco. Maybe it wasn't anything, just the ghosts of so many sleepless nights battling up the trail, tricking a man into crazy stunts.

Still he moved slowly, taking care to put each toe on solid ground, not making the slightest sound.

Might be more than one of them.

Couldn't see. Going up a slope, he could smell Kelly's cowchips smoldering. Was something there on the rock snout? A bush or a boulder, a cougar, or a man?

Something not the same color as the limestone slab it lay on. Would be a horse staked way back up yonder.

Cotton closed in carefully. He ignored his six-gun and the bowie, concentrating on getting in close to whatever it was.

Wasn't bush, wasn't boulder. It moved. Not much, but it moved.

Close to the edge, you make a dive on it, you liable to go over a hundred feet. Shake a man up some.

But as Cotton closed he realized there was no way out for whatever it was. It was trapped out there on the snout of rock, and the only way off was to go by old Cotton Dunbar, and Cotton's big hands were already tensed to take such a man apart.

How to do it quietly without setting the herd off?

Depended now on how much this thing wanted to fight. No way to tell from seeing a blob that'd twitch an arm or shift its head. Couldn't wait for moonrise. Cotton knew he was plumb tired. He couldn't just wait. He might go to sleep. Only way he could keep awake was to keep moving.

Keep moving. Be quiet, but move. Sure it was a man spread-eagled there on the limestone snout, listening and watching the dark camp below, wondering what was the matter. Why did they cut off the campfire? Why were they all shut up? From far out on the prairie you could hear the singing of a couple drowsy cowhands keeping their places, making up words that didn't make sense, just to jar them awake.

Right is right. Little ones make big ones. Cotton was on his belly squirming ahead like a lizard after a grasshopper, except anything moving makes some bit of noise, if only the creak of salt stiffened dungarees, and the thing there heard it, all right.

Too smart to just pull and fire, he played for a few seconds, getting off his belly and some weight on his toes and knees so he could move one way or another. Had a smoke pole of some kind alongside, and even as Cotton made his spring and dive, the other was squirming around, bringing up a shotgun, smacking the stock at Cotton's face, missing, catching a shoulder; but Cotton was already taking him to pieces with his big hands, one on his scrawny neck, the other after the elbow. Then the goddamned gun went off right next his ear, nearly blowing him off the cliff with sheer muzzle blast. Twisting it out of the scrawny thing's hand, the other hammer dropped and Cotton knew it then, not really thinking of the man in his hands at all, but preoccupied with the safety of the herd, already knew they'd be up and stampeding with that second blast, though it came up under the chin of the thing and blew brains, teeth, hair, eyeballs, and blood spray all over him; so even if he knew he ought to be running for a horse to turn the herd, he was laying off to one side, puking like a gorged buzzard and pawing at the burning mess on his face and hands. Kneeling there, retching it up, etching his teeth and blurring his thoughts, he felt the earth tremble, knew they were gone and wished them all kinds of luck.

The shock of hearing the earth rumble countered the spirit's horror. Given another couple seconds, Cotton stumbled to his feet and moved slowly, foot dragging, then faster and faster, until headlong he was coming down off the steep rocks and cutting around on a dead run toward camp where his horse should be waiting.

Good Lord, what a racket! All hands were out and scrabbling on their horses; even Kelly was on an old crowbait, heading out into the night. Somehow they all knew that if they could master this monster, they could coast all the way into Abilene, but Lordy, it was a big monster to fight for worn-out waddies.

No time to change boots, no time to wash off the offal, just leap to saddle and ride for the ruckus. He heard the crackling of longhorns clashing in wild panic, the heavy drumming of hooves, and the howl of riders waving lassoes to turn the mob into a mill, and then Cotton heard someone shooting. Not at cattle or stars, someone was shooting at the brave riders, already risking all.

An overpowering rage shook Cotton as he realized the abuse his people were taking, and forgetting cows and all, he rode directly toward the last gunflash he'd seen, and with his six-shooter out, caught two figures on horseback turning from his rush. Knowing not who they were, except they weren't his own, he dropped his big right hand and tucked in the first finger and let the bullet loose; and in an instant, again the dropping barrel, the tucking finger, the tearing explosion and the second rider dropping.

Not even stopping to look, Cotton turned his big gray around on a dime and busted back to the herd across prairie dog town, coulees, cutbanks, limestone slabs, anything or nothing, like it was all a dream.

Get to the point, turn it, keep it together so it didn't split and fan out. By daylight they'd see what was left. Into the line of his own riders he charged. They were keeping up the flanking sideways route, but the herd was slowly turning them instead of them turning the herd. It looked as if they were going to lose, seemed as if it was that one time where you had to kill your own stock, and his six-gun cracked and blew the lead bull backward into his mates, and as another surged on over, Cotton blasted him through the head so the others knew better than to turn against him, and just to make sure, he knocked down two more, laying them right into the side of the herd like little dams, forcing them into the left-hand turn they didn't want but had to take because there was a man wasn't going to let them do anything else. In a few minutes they'd gone into the mill where the leaders nosed up into the drag. Then Cotton pulled out wearily, sweat pouring off his lean-planed face, as the riders slowed them like a big clock winding down. In an hour they'd be bedded down again.

But God knew the cost.

9

Ardie and Wash stayed with the herd. They should have been strung out on the trail by sunup, but a cloud of anger and misery hung over the camp, and Cotton sat on his heels waiting for Cass to bring back the marshal if he could.

If he couldn't, they'd hold services and leave at noon, and Cass could catch up.

Five men were dead. There was the anger.

Cotton himself had killed three of them, and was sorry he hadn't got the others.

But the misery was to find the battered body of old Deef off in a coulee hung up in the stirrup of his wall-eyed horse. It wasn't the dragging that'd killed him, though, it was the bullet in his back.

Old Deef had sided Cotton when he first come to settle. A dried-up old sourpuss, he'd always been right where he was needed. Never said over a word a day, old Deef, but good Lord, didn't he ever do his best. Now to be shot like a coyote. Something real mean about that. You shouldn't never shoot a man who's already only half a step from being run over by two thousand red-eyed longhorns.

And Yancy. A young man, too young for the war but old as the hills in knowing his business and sticking up for himself. Tough little banty rooster, fight like a cat, anybody crowd him, but stuck with the outfit like it was his own kinfolk. He'd have rode through hell if Cotton said bring back some coals.

"He'd a made it except he had a big steer on to him anyways," blond, walrus-mustached Joe Benns said. "He was leaning over, smacking that steer on the snout with his rope end, shovin' that big sucker over with every step, and the one behind him and them behind him."

"I can see it," Cotton said quietly. "Goddamn it to hell, I can see it."

"Yonder behind us I seen the flash of a handgun and heard the shot. I seen him jump like he was jacked right out of the saddle, but there was half a dozen beeves between us. They carried me on their humps, right on by, couldn't get through. Made another swing and got in to him. 'Course, they'd been a hundred or so had tromped him by then."

"Sure." Cotton stared at the ground. "Sure."

Joe Benns chewed on his heavy mustache. "They didn't want to. I ain't mad at them beeves."

"I never even seen 'em," Stacey said.

"No sense playing it over again," Cotton said, "but I reckon this herd is worth more'n money now."

He saw two riders coming up from the south and recognized the long-legged chestnut Cass rode. The other would be that heavyset marshal.

"'Sposin' he's a Yankee lookin' for a reb to hang?" Chip put in.

"I guarantee you there's no marshal going to hang any of us out here," Cotton said. "If right isn't right, then we'll soon see what is."

As the marshal rode in, Cass dropped behind, changing horses from the remuda.

"Your man told me you had some losses," the big man said, dismounting from the broad-backed buckskin and facing Cotton directly.

"We did," Cotton said. "Two of the best men I ever rode with. They lost three in a fair fight."

He led the tall man to the five blanket-covered forms.

"This one is old Deef La Mont. Next is Yancy Carrol, a young hand. Both of 'em back-shot. Next three is them that picked the fight."

"Don't get on the prod, Mr. Dunbar. I seen you was a working drover when I come through late yesterday, and I got no ideas different since then. Somebody's got to report on this, though."

The marshal flipped aside the tarp covering the three dead rustlers.

"That one's been mighty close to a greener." The marshal swallowed, going through the pockets of the shattered men.

"It was his. He was their lookout."

"No way of identifying him, I guess," the marshal said. "Not that it's important. He's got a jackknife and small change in his pocket. You verify?"

"Yes," Cotton said, thinking sickly that this man was as poor as the rest of them. Poor men robbing poor men, killing each other. It didn't sound right.

"This next jasper," the marshal said, going through more pockets, "is some known, though he's got no price on his head I know of. A worthless skunk. He's got three ten-dollar gold pieces. This one here"—the marshal glanced an extra second at the stiffened, distorted features—"is a kid name of Doyle. All I know. Comes to town, blows his poke and drifts out. Had him in overnight for fighting drunk. He's got a dollar and a tin watch."

The marshal turned to Cotton. "Any family behind your two riders?"

"Deef was too old, and Yancy was an orphan." Cotton shook his head. "One was like an uncle to me, the other like a nephew, but neither one of 'em ever claimed any kin."

"Then I guess you better take this money and junk. If I take it, it means a lot of bookkeeping."

"Throw it away, then," Cotton said bitterly. "I wouldn't touch any of that with the tail end of my lassrope."

Going back to the cook wagon, he said to Kelly, "Dig a grave big enough for two."

Kelly started to ask about the other three, but after seeing the expression on Cotton's face, changed his mind. "Yessir," he said, rousting out a couple shovels from the wagon.

The marshal put the money and pocket goods into a salt sack, and helped himself to coffee.

"You can go any time," the marshal said, seeing the hole Kelly and Juan were digging. "Just two?"

"Mine I bury," Cotton said. "Them others can poison the varmints."

"Man's a man," the marshal said quietly.

"Right's right," Cotton said, motioning to Joe Benns, Stacey, Cass, Chip, Kelly, and Juan to gather with him.

They eased the blanket-wrapped bodies of their comrades into the hole side by side, and without any sermonizing, Cotton said, "They say the Boss will greet you Texas boys and he'll be leading gentle ponies for you. Whatever it is, Deef, damn. I sure hope it suits you, and Yancy, too."

He turned away, and big Kelly stood there kinda humming "Swing Low, Sweet Chariot," same as the boys had sung around the herd all the way north. He couldn't quite throw the dirt in without more ceremony, but nobody knew much, and so it was Joe Benns, his grizzled mustache prickling up angry, grabbed up a shovel and started throwing the dirt in, and Chip just pushed it in with his boot until everybody was pushing dirt in just to get it over.

Cotton rode out to Ardie and Wash with the herd. "You want to say a prayer over them graves, you can."

"Not me," Ardie said.

Wash thought it over longer. But he had about the same answer. "Let's get these goddamned critters to market. I'll say my prayer for old Deef and Yancy in Rosie's Barrel House."

"Good enough," Cotton said. Everybody had a chance to do what he wanted. He stood high in the stirrups and waved a circle with his sombrero.

"Move 'em out!" he called, slapping a big cow on the butt and crowding in on another little bunch, so they knew it was time to mosey on.

The rest of the hands picked their places and filled in the empty spots left by Yancy and Deef.

They'd only make five or six miles, but it'd get them out of the sorrowful ground. Looking back through the cloud of dust they raised, Cotton saw the marshal mounting his buckskin and looking on west.

By near dark they bedded down by a turgid creek that Cotton took to be a fork of the Smoky Hill River. He rode a large circle around the area and decided one man could handle the guard.

"Everybody bed down early," he said, swallowing a tough lump of steak. "I'm pretty fresh and so's my string. I'll give a call whenever I feel like dousin' down."

Nobody argued with him. Was no use arguing anyway with a man like him.

Cotton, beyond tiredness, rode along on a thin blue cloud, doing what habit told him to do, riding a slow circle over even ground around the bedded cattle, humming an old ballad. His thoughts weren't worth remembering. It was as if he were dreaming even as he made the long circle.

That precious herd would soon be tough beef for the Yankees. Their hides would make boots, and that would be it. Two men dead, the others worked to skin and bone for something that wouldn't even be there in a year. Only thing to keep was land. The ranch. Only thing that'd last. But you had to keep feeding the bank buzzards money or they'd move you out or kill you legal like.

Pay them off once and for all; never sign a paper again. Why? Why hang onto anything? God was too fickle to count on. To take Deef and Yancy in the same parcel just didn't make any sense at all unless it was a Great Plan to control the cowboy population.

If this creek was a feeder of the Smoky Hill, they were one day's distance from Abilene. They'd cross over by noon, be on the prairie by the railroad by sunset, and be in the pens, tallied, the next day.

Ardie rode out into the night without a call. Singing some fool song about Maybelle, he found Cotton going his circle, sound asleep, but sitting upright in his saddle, his horse walking gently as a rocking chair. Quietly Ardie led the pony and sleeping man back to camp and turned them over to Kelly.

As Ardie went on back to guard, he pictured the fandango he was going to have right soon.

> Oh, Maybelle, you're surely swell
> But you're not able for me to tell
> So please don't yell if I ring the bell
> While dancing the springs with Big-Nosed
>   Nell . . .

At daybreak Cotton was himself again. Somehow he'd gone past fatigue into a new feeling, as if he were floating in a tub of hot suds, but he was awake and moving. Not remembering how he'd come off guard, he didn't understand Ardie's wise cheeriness.

"Mornin', boss," Ardie said. "I bet you dreamed you was ridin' a horse last night."

"Didn't dream," Cotton said.

"Better eat your breakfast." Kelly winked at Ardie. "I got my chores to do."

Ardie took some corn pone and fatback, and washed it down with hot sugared coffee.

"You been out there all night?" Cotton asked as Ardie tossed the cup into Kelly's dishpan.

Ardie nodded. "Baying at the moon."

"Thanks. I'll take the right point, you can have the left. We'll cross the Smoky Hill River about noon."

To Kelly he said, "Make up a good dinner on the other side for the boys. Then we'll drift along slow while I check out Abilene. If they have room for us, we'll drive into the pens first thing in the morning."

"Suits me," Ardie said. "We'll ford the Smoky Hill easy."

"Easy, less'n there's a pile up of herds ahead of us."

"I can sure use a barber and a whole bath."

"Besides a drink or two," Chip said, his blond mustache slanting across a big smile.

"Just one for me. 'Course, Maybelle drinks like a hog." Ardie grinned. "How's about loanin' me a dollar till payday?"

"If you can make a dollar out of a dime, you're surely welcome to all I have," Chip said.

"We'll have money soon enough, boys, but I wish you'd let me hold back a stake for you," Cotton said. "There's no sense blowing it across a bar."

"Now, Captain," Ardie said, "Abilene needs the money."

"Texas needs it worse," Cotton said, stepping up in his stirrups, looking over the cattle.

They had a river to cross and about eight miles of unbroken prairie. By now, out of two thousand cattle, they knew 1900 by some name or mark or color. There's old Mailpouch. There's the red John, the black John, the grulla John, the spotted John, the milkin' Daisy, the bullin' Daisy, the dry Daisy, the splatterbutt Daisy . . .

They'd eaten thirty of the lame, halt, and blind, and a few strays picked up bearing foreign brands.

They'd lost two of their horses, but they'd picked up half a dozen off the Deveroo brothers.

On money they were even, starting with nothing and arriving with nothing.

The Smoky Hill River was low and the trail across its ford was tramped down solid. There were sandbars sticking up now, clotted with debris from the spring flood, and huge catfish were being trapped in the cut-off holes, and green scum was forming on the banks.

Wash kept the left swing, Chip had the right, and the drag was handled by Stacey and Joe Benns.

Hardly half a mile past the crossing, they saw fresh herd sign, and Cotton decided to ride on ahead. Could be some sort of a tangle, and no sense in driving two thousand mean-tempered cows into it.

Two miles took him to the edge of a bunch of cows branded Flat S. He didn't know the brand, but he knew it came from Texas.

He rode slowly into camp where some bristly bearded hands were playing poker for dry beans. Their greasy deck was near worn out on both sides.

"Howdy," Cotton said. "Boss around?"

"In town."

They were surly, cantankerous, salty.

"What's the wait? I'm from Bar D just south of here."

"No money, they claim. 'Course them eastern Yankees figured out any time you can screw a dollar out of a cowboy, go right ahead, he deserves it."

Tired as he was, Cotton felt the same nervous shiver he'd felt when Marshal Tosh had spoken of the potential problem.

Abilene had spread the word that it was the quickest

place to ship Texas beef from, had said, boy, howdy, they'd treat you right; and now, landing on their doorstep were thousands of cattle and hundreds of cowpunchers wanting what they'd come for.

"They have shipping pens?"

"Sho 'nough," another of the bitter-faced men said, sneering. "Empty and waitin'. Whyn't you just drive your stock on in."

Cotton touched his hat and turned his mount toward the town, a town that hadn't even been there until Joy McCoy settled that mark on the map as being a shipping point.

Every couple miles another herd grazed and the grass was wearing thin. Another day or so, they'd be having to drift back farther west.

Cotton decided there was no point in stopping at each outfit. The answer was in Abilene. He had the telegram from Oglethorpe in his oilskin wallet, and Oglethorpe should be there with an answer.

He passed by five separate herds. Roughly twelve thousand cattle, and Cotton knew there were more coming up the trail behind his own. They'd be piling in on his tail. Should be cars hauling these critters east. Should be rolling a herd east as fast as another came in. Something crossbuck somewhere.

Abilene was two blocks long and one block wide. Its street was planted to alfalfa once maybe, but it was tromped out from mud into dust, and the buildings along each side were gray-brown from the street dirt.

Smoky Hill National Bank was the only stone building in town. Had to walk up three steps. Give you a feeling of going into something important.

He didn't usually like towns anyway, but there was something extra fly-blowed and foundered about this one. Seemed like it was deader'n salt horse. Nobody doing anything. Couple old scruffy loafers chewing at the storefront with their round heels. Couple old dogs sleeping front of the Mercantile, hoping the butcher'd throw out a bone.

Couple horses hip-shot at the hitch rail in front of the Yellow Daffodil Saloon. They looked as if they were shills posted out there to make it look like somebody was inside.

His stomach tightening up, he tied his mount at the iron hitchrail in front of the bank. Should be the sound of trains moving cattle cars out, cowboys drunk in the middle of the afternoon, raising all kinds of houlihan, and a hundred horses tied up at the empty rails.

Should be a half a dozen clean-dressed and fleshed-out cattlemen standing around the bank, pockets full of greenbacks, and yarning quiet like.

Nobody. Just ghosts that hadn't even got there yet. A dust devil spinning down the middle of the street.

He walked up the three limestone steps to the glass and brass door. Just looking inside, it seemed closed. Nobody there. His belly tighter'n wrung-out rawhide, he shoved on the door and was half surprised when it opened.

Inside, dank and dry and dismal. Like all banks. Used money smells like that, he thought. Kind of dirty and mildewed. They never get rid of that smell.

He stepped to a grilled window and found a bald-headed clerk standing there, cleaning his nib pen.

"Yes, sir," the clerk said.

"I'm looking for Mr. Oglethorpe. Chester Oglethorpe."

"Your name?"

"Cotton Dunbar. Bar D, Texas."

"Step this way, please," the clerk said politely, if distantly, as if he'd said the same thing to a dozen Cotton Dunbars that very morning.

Cotton walked down to the end of the room, passed inside the counter and was shown into the office of the banker.

"Mr. Dunbar, sir," the clerk said to the man sitting at his desk nodding sleepily.

Cotton waited for the big, stocky man to greet him. But Oglethorpe only looked at him bitterly, then looked away and pushed a fat hand at a chair. "Sit down, Mr. Dunbar."

Cotton came to the point. "What's wrong?"

"You haven't heard?" Oglethorpe suddenly looked back at Cotton.

"Haven't heard anything, haven't even got to bedground yet. But there's five herds out yonder waitin'. I got to know where to put mine and how long before we ship."

"Mr. Dunbar," Oglethorpe said heavily, "I'm glad you know you aren't the only one."

"I got your telegram," Cotton said.

"Sure," the fat man said sourly, "but I sent you another one a little later. Maybe you didn't get it."

"No, sir, we were gone. What's the problem?"

"Problem in a nutshell is there isn't any money anywhere. Something happened in the market back east. A crash. Panic. Money panic. Every dime is hid and set on. We can't get a penny."

"I don't understand high finance," Cotton said carefully. "I do understand cows and a man's promise."

"Certainly. But this one time there is no money.

Not just from me, not just from Abilene, or the railroad. There isn't any money anywhere."

"You mean your contract is no good?"

"I mean I can't hardly buy a cigar till the easterners sort themselves out."

"But you, you're the one I'm dealin' with, not anybody back east. I mean I have your wire, and I took you at your word."

"You aren't alone, like I said."

"No, sir, it's you and me. Nobody else. I lost two of the best riders ever come out of Texas to do it. And I expect you to keep your word."

Oglethorpe's skin was changing colors from red to gray to purple, and sweat beaded his face. These dumb drovers were all alike. They wouldn't understand it wasn't his fault that Wall Street was busted and the price of beef was a goose egg in Chicago.

"Mr. Dunbar, believe me, as soon as the money comes in, as soon as credit is reestablished and currency liquid, as soon as anything changes for the better, you'll find my word is good as gold."

"You have the money in the vault?"

"The money in the vault isn't mine, it's the bank's and earmarked as reserves."

"Sir, the date was July first, and that's all there is to it."

"You think I'm trying to defraud you?"

"Just tell me when to bring my herd into the pens and collect my money."

"My guess is you can bring the herd in and ship it anytime you feel like it, but you'll only get the market price, and that won't even pay the freight."

"Then I understand you have lied to me," Cotton said, standing, not red-hot angry, just worn out. He felt like a mad prodded bull who's been pushed so far he sulls. "My hands will feel the same as me."

"Best thing I can tell you is charge a few bottles at the Daffodil to me, and take them back to camp."

"I reckon I ain't down to jawbone liquor yet," Cotton said. "I'll be back here day after tomorrow at noon. My herd'll be ready to ship, and I'll expect $62,700. That's thirty-three dollars a head, as we agreed in San Antone." Cotton cut the total price to account for the beeves lost on the drive.

"You better believe me, Mr. Dunbar, there ain't a thousand dollars loose west of the Mississippi. I'm not disputing the price, but there simply is not, understand, is not, any cash money anywhere we know of."

"A contract is a contract. And right is right."

Oglethorpe trembled more from rage than fear. Of all the mossybacked, cantankerous Texas cattlemen who'd come in and been faced with the same problem, this tall man with the gray eyes and the big hands looked to be the most formidable. He was one of the simple kind—yes, no, black, white, will, won't, wet, dry, kill, die.

Best thing was to settle down and cool off and understand there wasn't any money. No money to spend, leastwise.

10

Yet of all the cattlemen Oglethorpe had faced and explained the tightness of money too, none understood the situation better than Cotton Dunbar.

He knew money went by rules, and the rules were made by the banker, like dealer's choice in cards, and that's why the banker and the dealer always got richer, and anybody trying to buck the game found himself out on the seat of the pants in a short time. Cash money moving around depended on everybody trusting that it was worth what they said it was. But when folks decided there wasn't anything to trust, they hung onto their money. The money was there, it was the trust that was missing.

Meant they'd eat beans instead of beef, until there was so much beef piled up you could get it for nothing. The ultimate victim of money panics was always the farmer or the cattlemen.

Cotton decided the telegram was just as good as

money. Maybe it was Oglethorpe's mistake, but for sure it wasn't the Bar D's. Bar D did just what it was supposed to do and some extra. Banker never gave anything extra; it was always the big-hearted and hardworking, rope-burned and saddle-callused cattlemen who gave out the favors, always setting up the drinks, or throwing in something to boot.

No, Oglethorpe had the money, all right; bankers all over the country had it, but they was scared to spend it. Waiting for the big stud banker in New York City to give the nod. You could sell that snake-oil money talk to bullwhackers, grangers, and knot-headed cowpunchers, but you couldn't make it pour water out of a boot for Cotton Dunbar.

His only question was how to cash in the telegram.

Maybe Oglethorpe would ride out and make a privy deal, knowing how Cotton felt about things. That would be accommodating.

Cotton was hardly aware he'd taken the rein off the hitchrail and swung into the saddle. When he had said, "I'll be back day after tomorrow with my herd ready to ship, and I'll be expecting to receive $62,700," he meant it.

The only way. The right way. Fat, cigar-smoking schemers in their walnut-paneled offices didn't top out anybody on the Bar D, because Cotton Dunbar was the ramrod, and when it came down to right or wrong, big or small, hang tight or fall out, Cotton was boss. Everybody else that came along took hind tit.

Bankers included.

There was a vault in that bank. On the window of the bank a sign said in gold leaf, NET RESERVES $700,000. To Cotton that meant the bank had to carry no less than ten percent of that figure in their vault. Maybe more, but no less. Ten percent of $700,000 was about what they owed him.

He turned the big buckskin and trotted him right back the way he came. First things first. You don't just drive your herd through the bank's plate-glass window. It might take a little time to get all the loose ends straightened out, and it was right to let Oglethorpe know he couldn't weasel out. Right now he'd be shaking like a leaf and thinking about absconding to San Francisco.

Shorthanded, still the drovers were where Cotton expected them to be. He rode across the right flank of the herd, nodded to the riders as they slowly walked the herd westerly. He judged he could have the whole herd into the Abilene pens in four hours driving time, and the nearest herd to him on the prairie was three miles east. It would take a hell of a lightning bolt to get them mixed up, and the weather looked good.

The low, wailing wind from the northwest persisted and sang its haunting tunes, but there was no storm or electricity in it.

All that was lacking to make the drive a success was collecting the money and getting it back to the people in Texas so's they could pay back their mortgages. Seemed almost like a national scheme, didn't it, to squeeze out the working men. Banker on one end won't pay, banker on the other end forecloses for default of payment. They don't default Cotton Dunbar, he thought, not when he does what's right.

The beef looked good. They ought to, the way he'd mothered and brooded over every one of them, broke his leg and killed seven men.

No money! Good Lord, how could you bare-faced tell that to a man just bringing in his drive? No money? Well, then, I'll take blood; not all the blood, just enough blood to pay for Deef and Yancy. That's not much, though of course it gets to be quite a lot if it's yours.

Cotton sat on a blanket roll, staring at the little cookfire, ignoring the anxious looks of Kelly, slowly laying back on the coarse wool blanket, thinking it gets to be pretty high-priced when it's in your own blood, Mr. Oglethorpe, but if that's the new tender of exchange, you owe me two lives and a broke leg that ain't ever goin' to be right again . . .

Juan had taken the boss's buckskin without a word, like always, but seeing everything with those black, quick eyes.

Looking at his boss's face, he saw the grayness, the bone-tired exhaustion, and the powerful disappointment he'd brought back with him. He knew then without speaking it even in his mind that it was big trouble and it would grind on everyone in the outfit.

He took the buckskin to the remuda and turned him out with hobbles like the rest of the horses. They wouldn't be going anywhere for a while.

Kelly fussed over pots and pans. Boss didn't bring nothing back from town. Could've brought some peppercorns, could've brought fresh flour, could've brought some apples, but he didn't bring nothing, just that faraway look in his eyes, like they was thick glass set in lead casings. Maybe it was just the end-of-the-road weariness, but surely he'd've thought to bring a few potatoes, or some dried peas from town. But nothing. Nothing at all. Just plain-out nothing at all. Kelly was singing it in his head.

Boss didn't bring back nothin', nothin' at all,
Went to town but he didn't bring nothin' back,
Boss didn't bring nothin', not even a peppermint
Not even a lick of molasses, not even a slab of
    bacon,
Ain't it a fact,
He didn't bring nothin' at all.

Tight-faced, Ardie had heard the boss say, "Hold
'em here, two guards," and ride on without another
word. Not a syllable of cheer, not a turned-up smile,
not a flash of winning joy.

'Course, he's tired, who ain't? But if it'd gone right
in town, he'da showed something. If he'd brought
back a box of seegars, or a bottle of Old Crow to pass
around. But all he brought back was a blue-ice look in
his eyes, and a little stiffer ramrod in his neck bones.

It wasn't right and it boded sorrow, and Ardie
wouldn't let his dog's uncle touch sorrow. Ardie kept
sorrow away like it'd poison your blood. He'd given
up on sorrow, ever since he lost Amy. Amy was sort of
the virtuous sister of Maybelle, because Amy liked to
laugh just like Ardie. Could laugh like a little tinkling
pool in a green ferny dell with a bluejay squawkin'
above, and, oh, that's all there was to bring back.
Whenever that sort of a little memory poked its head
up, he'd yell "Maybelle, come over here and let me set
in your lap and ease the blisters on my poor old
rawed-out hoolihan!

"Oh my, Maybelle, bring me a sup of water and
pour it with your rosy lips!

"Maybe you go see the boss, Maybelle, tell him old
Ardie needs a few coins for our pleasure. I buy you a
drink, Maybelle, I buy you lots of pretty drinks, green

ones and red ones, blue ones and yeller ones and rainbow-stripedy ones and polky-dotty drinks, and fat drinks and skinny drinks and drinks with bubbles in 'em and drinks with sorghum in 'em, and dry drinks and wet drinks and flowery drinks and stinkin' drinks, whoo-ee, I tell you, Maybelle, hurry up with a few of them gold coins because this here is one cowboy ready for to paint his nose!"

Come morning light, every manjack of them had had himself nine, ten hours of sleep, and most of them felt as if they'd been hammered blind with an oak maul. Cotton felt the fur in his mouth, and cleared his throat and grabbed for the coffee.

"Dang, I don't know if I can stand the pace," Chip said, clutching his knees and scratching his long, curly beard.

"Feel like I been drug through every tunnel in prairie-dog town by the head dog hisself," Joe Benns groaned.

Cotton glanced at the crew, noting that Wash and Ardie were gone, and across the prairie the two riders sat slow-moving horses at opposite edges of the grazing herd. The grass was good, and there was miles of it open; they could probably set out the rest of the summer right here if they had to, only his note was due in August, and so was Penny's and the rest. Suppose his banker would settle for an excuse that there wasn't no money? Cotton smiled to himself bitterly. Not by a long shot; bankers didn't ever accept excuses—they just accepted the collateral.

He chewed on a biscuit and a hunk of fried beef, trying not to show the prickling fear that was running up the middle of his backbone.

"See to the relief, and keep the herd easy," Cotton said to Cass. "I'm goin' to call on our neighbors."

"When do we ship?" Stacey asked, still rubbing the sleep out of his eyes.

"Not settled yet," Cotton said truthfully.

"How come?" Stacey asked sharply.

"Takes time," Cotton replied easily, moving off to the remuda, where he chose a black gelding because his back was unmarked.

Swinging up and riding out, Cotton saw in one glance that the camp was trim, the beef bunched loose enough to feed easy but tight enough to keep an eye on each and every critter.

He rode upriver, noting the condition of the grass and the flow of the stream. He could see driftage in the cottonwoods, high as his head where the spring floods had touched and left their mark, but now the river was far down in its banks and flowing too slowly to even see a ripple of motion. Another month and there might be only puddles and mucky sloughs, but he'd be back in Texas trying to put something together.

It hit him hard just then. Maybe because he'd had sleep enough to make his spirit sensitive again, maybe it was just the way the grass waved under the wind and the cottonwoods twinkled in the morning light. He never could think of why it should strike at any special time, all he could think of was the remembrance of his little wife holding the baby boy, trying to mother him against all harm, remembering how she looked, her chin atremble like a cottonwood leaf, with the babe in her arms because they all could sense the moment of destiny; and God knows he could not, did not, augur the future from that terrible moment when in somber dignity he'd mounted his big black horse and rode off to defend something called freedom from the Yanks.

And they were dead while he was dragging back off Malvern Hill, while the battles were being won but the war was being lost.

"Freedom? Oh, Lord!" he groaned aloud. "I'm sorry. If I had stayed to home I couldn't have faced the soldier boys comin' back, nor the kin of those that didn't, but if I hadn't gone, at least I'da been with my own when their hour struck, and maybe just one man and one rifle might've made the difference."

Put it away, put it away, he told himself. It's done, put it away. There's no way out of that pit but down. Think on something, think on Penny Dickinson. She got the same remorse only the other way, seeing her man swell up and die in agony.

It would all go away in a minute if he could think on bankers and cattle and land.

He rode now among cattle, longhorns much like his own, except they seemed taller, rangier. Now they fed like they'd not eaten in three months, or three years for that matter, because there was no pasture as rich as this anywhere in Texas.

Their heads hardly left the ground, so busy were their tough mouths wrapping up the grass. Their bellies were stretched tight as if they were cows about to freshen, but they were gant-legged steers who were just as apt to founder themselves with bloat as not. Somebody should be keeping them moving slow enough so's they'd have to take a breath between bites. But there was only one rider and he was setting his pony far across the herd. He had one leg hung over his saddle horn, smoking a pipe. The cattle divided as

TEXAS RULES

Cotton worked his way over toward the motionless rider.

The rider nodded as he approached, but he didn't uncock his leg or take the pipe out of his mouth.

"Howdy, I'm Cotton Dunbar from the herd just east of you."

The man nodded and at last removed the pipe and said, "Bill Gentry. These 'uns is mine. Come up from Goliad two weeks ago."

"You aren't alone?" Cotton asked. "None of my business, I guess," he added. He had no intention of prying, but he'd had that terrible prescience that here were two thousand steers with one man watching them.

"I am. My hands drifted off. Couldn't pay 'em. Don't blame 'em for cuttin'. They busted their tails for me, figurin' at least they was goin' to be paid a wage when they got done. I couldn't make the payroll, so they left."

"Couldn't sell the beef?"

"Ain't you heard?"

"About the money panic back east? Sure, I heard that. But it don't mean nothin' to a cowboy with a herd of steers that never stop eating."

"I been studyin' on that for at least nine days now," the grizzled rider said, poking the pipe into his dry lips and drawing on it to get it going again.

"No answer to it?"

"Banker won't pay out money, I won't deliver the beef. Somethin's got to happen."

"What?"

"Only thing I can figure is to cut out a little bunch, maybe a hundred head at a time, drive 'em east, and

115

sell 'em to the grangers a head at a time. Trade 'em for somethin', I dunno, but get rid of 'em."

"Not enough time."

"I'll let you have 'em for fifteen dollars a head."

"They're worth thirty."

The chunky rider sucked his pipe, not wanting to talk about the subject anymore. He'd studied it nine days straight, and there wasn't an answer, any more than there was an answer to an earthquake or a prairie fire.

"I'll let you have 'em for fifteen, and no cash down. Just paper payable on your honor in Texas within a year or two."

"Sorry," Cotton said. "I got my own herd to sell."

"We're licked by the damn yankees again," Bill Gentry said.

"Rest of the drovers on around feel the same way?" Cotton asked.

"Some are willing to sell if they can get a dollar a head above freight. 'Course, they lose their ranches that way."

"I'm in the same box," Cotton said. "Me and my neighbors."

"Well, we've seen hard times before," Gentry said. "I guess we'll make it through another one."

"If we can give you a hand, Mr. Gentry, let me know."

"Much obliged, Mr. Dunbar," Gentry said. "If I knew what to ask for, I'd ask, I reckon."

Cotton turned the black horse back the way he'd come. Was no point in going on and hearing more doom and desperation.

The morning was clear and bright, like yesterday

morning, but there was a dismal bayou smell to it already.

Going to have to make that banker, Oglethorpe, stand by his word.

He resisted the little flurry of panic that tried to cry out inside him that the banker would smile him to hell, or would talk him to death, but never give over a penny of what he'd promised. No, this was a thing bigger than any man. It come up to the same kind of principles a man goes to war for. He fights for his own freedom and he fights for his own rights.

The big horse picked his way back at his own pace as Cotton grappled with the problems.

He was damned if he was going to belly-up like old Gentry. He wasn't going back home whipped like a yeller dog. He was going to be paid as per contract. He was going to try to do it peaceable.

And the little bug inside him asked, "Suppose Banker Oglethorpe don't do it? Are you goin' to belly up peaceable?"

If Mr. Oglethorpe needs any help staying on the straight and narrow, maybe I'll have to help him, Cotton admitted to himself without smiling.

Was no point in chewing the cabbage with the crew until there was something solid to it. For now they thought payday was right soon and were gettin' themselves in the proper jolly spirit.

In camp, Ardie stretched out in the shade of the chuckwagon, reeving a thong of buckskin through the broken sole of his boot.

"Come on, old boot, you done made it all the way from New Orleans, you can make it another couple miles to Abilene," Ardie admonished the wrinkled, scraped, and battered boot. "Won't be long and I'm goin' to set you free, goin' to get me a set of shiny, star-heeled stovepipes with white eagles and diamonds sewed on 'em. Goin' to get me some stripedy-duck pants and a purty silky shirt, and might be if they's five dollars left, I might just put on a new sombrero, whether I need it or not."

He grinned as he regarded the raddle-brimmed, grease-caked, and torn-peaked hat. "I bet that hat could put on these boots and walk away." He laughed.

"You know, Ardie, they's girls in Abilene. I can smell 'em clean out here," Chip drawled.

"Why sure they's girls in Abilene!" Ardie declared. "Wherever there's cowboys in town, there's always girls! Why shouldn't there be? After all, the manliest men anywhere, bar none, is cowboys! Ain't any two-legged hombre alive can match up the generosity, good looks, honorable intentions, and honest-to-God equipage a cowboy can bring to the girls. I mean what else would a good, fun-lovin' girl ever want than a good fun-lovin' cowboy!"

"Oh, Lordie, I just can't wait!" Cass howled, anticipating the glorious event when he'd be swept into the arms of a perfumed female.

It was a fact, they'd rode themselves to being just plain bones and hard muscles, rode themselves to the raw point where they was just all male, one hundred percent aching, raging, crazy manhood, and any pillowy, long-haired, roundy, soft and silky lady was the target, the nest, the irresistible magnet that pulled with merciless joy.

"Me neither," Ardie said. "Good gracious, I remember big-eared, fatbacked Lucille! Oh, wasn't she a dove on the wing? Wasn't she a downy, sweet bird made just for Ardie's pleasure! Sorry, Maybelle, sometimes a man can't control his animal instincts."

"Dang it, I wish't you'd quit talkin' about all that nauch and stuff, I can't hardly bear the waitin' no more." Joe Benns groaned, staring off at the general direction of Abilene with lovesick, mournful eyes.

"You suppose they have girls of color?" Wash asked.

"Don't you worry, Wash," Ardie said, "they got girls any color you want. When it comes to cowboys, girls check his temperature before they check his sunburn."

"Get ready, Wash." Cass laughed. "You'll get your wick dipped and go broke along with the rest of us."

"I just want a little bit."

"You wasn't a friend of mine, I'd call you a liar, 'cause you look to me like you goin' to try to wear it out."

"No, I know better'n that." Wash flashed a bright smile. "It just seems to muscle up the more you work at it."

"Ooo-eee!" Ardie howled, "Maybelle, where you now when I need you most!"

Looking off, Cass murmured, "Maybe that's her comin' yonder."

All eyes turned toward the distant riders. Two men, just coming on steady, straight for camp.

"Captain," Ardie said to Cotton, who'd schooled himself to ignore the ongoing dry mirth, "couple visitors."

Cotton was writing a letter, and he hated to write letters. But once started, he hated more to quit, like a man just having jumped into a cold bath and called out again. Somebody had to let Penny Dickinson know what was happening. It was only fair to tell her how it was up here so's she didn't get her hopes up too high, and besides, he'd promised to write when they made the railhead anyways.

"Dear Mrs. Dickinson," (he wanted to call her Penny, but Dear Penny didn't look right. She might think he was trying to be familiar):

The herd arrived here in good shape. We lost two good men, Deef and Yancy, in a stampede by rustlers. Which we took care of. Now we're here on bedground waiting to tally and sell. There's money problems back east, and them folks think they can pass it on to us. I mean to get what's due. But don't spend it yet, as it could be bust for all.

He didn't say that if it was a bust, he wouldn't bother to take the ride home.

For sure Penny wouldn't want to see him, poor as a churchmouse and having lost her money along with that of the rest of the folks in the valley, so's this just might be the last letter and word he'd have for her, and he wanted somehow to say that, but didn't know how to turn the words to his meaning.

This would be Oglethorpe making his call.

He put the letter back into the leather-bound note case, along with the steel-nibbed pen.

Might be there'd be no call to even write of bad news. Might be all over in an hour. He didn't feel near as much on the prod. A night's sleep could do wonders for a man's outlook. Wonder he hadn't done something foolish yesterday, bone tired and sandy-eyed mean as he was from the drive. Today he felt cool and calm, maybe a little worried, but his head was clear and any judgment he made would be responsible and right.

The other rider was familiar, but Cotton had to wait until they were nearly into camp before he recognized Marshal Tosh who'd come through at Crystal Springs.

———————— **11**——

It didn't look so good, banker bringing along the law. You get a combination like that and the poor man is bound to find himself squeezed. Still, law was law, supposed to protect everybody equal. No matter how much or how little property he had, it was supposed to be equal. And Cotton believed in that principle right to the bottom of his backbone. It was the equality of justice that made right right. So's if you were wrong, then you took your medicine. And if you were right, you took what was coming to you.

He waited until they dismounted before speaking, and by then the crew had managed to find enough odd jobs to disappear. All except Kelly, who brought out three mugs and a pot of coffee before saying he had to go fetch some firewood down at the creek bottom.

"Howdy, Marshal," Cotton said easy like, "and Mr. Oglethorpe. Set and take your ease."

They looked at him as if he was a new type of alligator. He was too smooth, and too tough.

"Marshal come along . . ." Oglethorpe hesitated over the words.

"To protect our money?" Cotton asked.

"Well, not exactly, mainly just to understand the regrettable situation."

"Umm," Cotton murmured, giving nothing.

"I mean, you said you was driving in tomorrow. I figured it best you knew the consequences of such a rash act."

"Do I look like a rash man, Marshal?" Cotton asked easily.

"A man can look one way and be another. Depends on how hard he's rode," Tosh said, almost warmly, like he'd just feel fine if'n he could gun down the big Texan for one reason or another.

Cotton wouldn't play their game. He meant to play his, because his was simple and in the right. Wasn't nothing wiggly or squirmy about his side of it.

"I figure you're here to protect my interests, Marshal. If you're not, you might as well haul your butt back to town."

"I'm here to make sure they ain't trouble," Tosh said uneasily.

"Ain't goin' to be trouble if'n Mr. Oglethorpe here does what he promised."

"I told you there isn't any money loose. It isn't just me, Mr. Dunbar, there is no money in Salina or Kansas City, or Chicago, or New York City. It's locked up and it's not moving."

"You reckon the banker in Texas holds my mortgage will pay any mind to that when due date comes?"

"Depends," Oglethorpe said, "maybe you can plead for more time."

"Plead?" Cotton's voice deepened into a shudder-

ing rasp. "Anybody pleadin' is goin' to be the somebody who owes me my money and not payin' up."

"That's where I come in," Tosh interrupted. "We
know you Texicans is all shaggy and salty, but you still
ain't goin' to ride roughshod over Kansans."

"Wrong, Marshal," Cotton said, keeping his face
composed and his voice back to an easy drawl. "I'm
peaceable. All of us are. But we aren't goin' to roll over
and waggle our tails when somebody tries to renege on
his word."

"You've talked to the others?" Oglethorpe asked.

"I talked to Gentry. But he didn't have a paper from
you. I held off startin' up the trail till I was sure you
knew what I aimed to do and what your end of our
bargain was."

"I guess you could take it to court." Tosh grinned.
"Judge might come by about the end of August."

"Tosh, you tryin' to get me riled up?" Cotton held
him with his frosty-blue eyes. "I don't recommend it.
I don't move till I'm sure I'm right."

"I'm the one says what's right. Not you."

"That's your second mistake, Marshal!" The big
Texan took a quick step forward, his eyes fixed on
Tosh, his hand next to his Navy Colt, his voice
hammering. "You don't tell me what's right. Govern-
ment scum like you, serving like a hired pissant for no
cause exceptin' the peedunky power and wages don't
mean a damn to me. You want to have it out, let's get
at it!"

Tosh crouched, his face burning red, while the
fire-tipped words of the standing Texan stung him like
a string of hornets.

"Just a second. Let's have no hard feelings," Oglethorpe said quickly. "We can all live with reason or we can suffer the consequences of violence."

"I agree on that, Mr. Oglethorpe," Cotton said, keeping his eyes on the Marshal, his hand next to the walnut butt of his forty-four. "You shouldn't have brought this brag along with you. There'd been less chance of a mix-up."

"I'm here to keep you from jumping Mr. Oglethorpe."

"You're here to protect the innocent, and keep the peace. If'n you ain't, get out of my camp," Cotton said.

Again the marshal flushed red and let his hand hover over the butt of his six-gun.

"Easy now, Mr. Dunbar's right. All we want is peace and reason," Oglethorpe said.

"I mean to drive my herd into the pens tomorrow morning." Cotton glanced at the banker. "I expect you to have thirty-three dollars a head cash ready for me when the tally's done."

"Impossible," Oglethorpe snapped. "I'm done telling you. There's no money. Nobody's buying, nobody's selling."

"I'll count 'em for you, Mr. Oglethorpe. And I'll expect the money right at noon."

"Crazy," Tosh said disgustedly. "Mule-headed crazy."

"I think I'm the only one here that's still tellin' it exactly the way it is. You know it. Mr. Oglethorpe knows it, and I know it. It ain't like an Injun treaty, it's a man's word."

"But circumstances . . ." Oglethorpe tried again, but seeing the calm face, the piercing eyes, the set, stubborn jaw, knew it was useless. "C'mon, Tosh. You better raise up a posse to guard the town."

"I'm not after war. I wouldn't ask my boys to fight for the money any more'n I'd ask somebody else to protect it. Best just pay it over and be done with it."

"You better turn around and go back to Texas," Tosh said. "And take your damned cows along with you."

"I guess you don't hear me," Cotton said softly.

Oglethorpe glared at Cotton silently, shoved a newspaper into his hand and said, "You fool. Read this."

He mounted his horse and rode back toward town with the marshal coming up behind him.

For the first time Cotton felt the prickly cold that meant he was unsure of himself, that maybe right wasn't right after all. Maybe the law was not law. Maybe business was thievery. Maybe the gun was the only way of honor. No, no. He shook it off. They'll see the light. We'll make the drive into the pens and I'll call for the money and Oglethorpe will pay it.

Ardie came around from the back of the chuckwagon. He wasn't smiling. He wasn't calling on Maybelle for help, he was holstering his six-gun.

Kelly had a big butcher knife in his hand, wiping it on his sack apron. Cass and Joe were mounted, ready to relieve the other riders, but they had their saddle guns couched across their laps, and the others seemed to be spotted here and there, looking in a way guilty, and in another way as wicked, savage, salty as any pack of timber wolves ever to bust down the Missouri Breaks.

"Couldn't help hearin' it, boss," Ardie said. "You folks was raisin' your voices."

"Forget what you heard. We're goin' to do what we

126

started out to do. Won't be any bloodshed, won't be anything illegal. If we deliver, he's *got* to pay up, not because we have the guns, not because we can fight as good as most anybody, but because we're plain wide-out open in the *right!* Now forget the guns. You're just lookin' for excitement. I don't blame you, and if it works out like I say, you'll have it on Railroad Avenue tomorrow night."

"Either way," Ardie said, "we're goin' to have it."

"We're not goin' off half-cocked. Believe me."

"Seems like this may be outside your loop," Cass said. "Seems like it's our concern, too."

"I'm supposed to see to our cattle in case somethin' comes up too big for you to handle." Young Stacey stepped forward as if his hour of glory had come.

"If you care anything about your sister, you'd best quieten down and use your head." Cotton struggled to hold his temper.

"Well, I sure say this—you didn't back off none from 'em." Joe Benns laughed.

"We're all in it together, Captain," Ardie said with such quiet simplicity they all knew it was the cold, unrevocable truth.

"Yes, 'Course we are. From the day we started north," Cotton said, thinking of Deef and Yancy Carrol. "But I'm not having more dead friends on my conscience. You boys get feisty, you'll go it alone."

"We goin' to follow your lead," Ardie said, "but we ain't goin' to be far behind."

"Best relieve the guard," Cotton said, "and let's get ready for the drive tomorrow. Plenty to do. Anybody got spare time, he can help Juan shoe the ponies."

The men went to work, while Cotton unfolded the newspaper Oglethorpe had thrust into his hand.

The Kansas City Star. Lots of headlines atop each column of print. All about the tariff and the new bridge and the murder, but the one on the right said, MISERY DEEPENS IN THE EAST AS PANIC WORSENS.

Thousands of unemployed lined up this morning for a bowl of broth and a piece of bread from relief soup kitchens set up at the President's urgent request. The streets are crowded day and night with men and women evicted from their homes for lack of rent payment. John Vanderbilt was unavailable for comment, but a spokesman said it is believed the worst is over and the laws of supply and demand should soon take hold once more.

Seasoned observers see no sign of relief from the economy's downward spiral. Unemployed workers are on the rise, building construction is at a standstill. Steel mills in Pennsylvania are closing more hearths . . . Congressman Chase calls for reform of the Chartered Bank system . . .

To read the article made a situation far away seem believable. You could see the lines of shabby folks waiting for a cup of soup, see the banker Vanderbilt deep in his walnut-paneled office, unavailable for comment, see the evictions from flats, see the steel mills close their gates, and the politicians crying out for reform. Sure, you could see it all there in the dark brick cities, but for the life of him, Cotton couldn't understand it out here in the middle of Kansas, where the tallest building counting its false front was maybe twelve feet, and there were more soup bones walking around than you could count, and the sun was shining hot, and fleecy clouds floated overhead the way they always did in summertime over the Big Pasture.

He put the paper in his saddlebag. Might be useful to wrap something in some day.

Cotton mounted the black and rode off toward the grazing cattle. Their feet were healed. The weak-legged ones were standing better and limping less. Ornery old brindle John was a little ornerier, tossing up dust with his front feet to drive off the flies and announce his own cantankerousness.

You're goin' to be a soup bone soon, John, boy, Cotton thought. You too damned old and tough for beef.

All in all, it was a fair-looking herd of critters. Some poor, some old, but they balanced it out with some good fat three-year-olds. They weren't wormy or grubby, weren't scarred up bad, weren't sick with fever or blackleg, weren't crazy from loco or jimson, were just a good, average herd of honest beeves ready for market, and come daybreak they'd make their last walk across grass.

He came abreast Ardie, who'd relieved Wash Washington.

"Satisfied?" Ardie asked.

"Look fine to me. We put the extra work into keeping them up, and it shows."

"Weather's good, won't thunder for a week. Shouldn't be nothin' around to bother them tonight."

Ardie was always chattering like a cricket, but once in a while he said things ought to be said.

"Why'd you say that?" Cotton asked.

"What?"

"Shouldn't be nothin' bother'n 'em tonight?"

"Shouldn't, of course. What is there?"

129

"But why didn't you say wouldn't or won't or can't nothin' bother 'em tonight?"

"'Cause there ain't . . . Oh, good Lord . . ."

"You're smarter'n you know," Cotton said bleakly. "Let's move the herd and set us a wolf trap."

"You think that banker . . . the marshal . . . those bastards!"

"Why not? They sure as hell don't want to see us in the mornin'."

"And I be danged if I'm goin' to chase these steers one more time."

"Start movin' 'em southwest," Cotton said, standing tall in his stirrups and looking over the terrain. "We might as well play it our way if we got to play it."

"Maybelle, put your dress back on, I got to go to work," Ardie hooted.

"If we can hold to the other side of that knob and put Juan up there with a campfire, it might obfuscate them enough to make a bad move."

"I'll get 'em started." Cotton signaled across the herd to Cass and rode quickly around to the northeast to turn and drift the herd slowly to another place where they wouldn't ordinarily be.

Cotton told the plan to Cass in three sentences and Cass's face dropped.

"By damn it, I'm plumb out of patience with these folks," he declared, and snapped the end of his lassrope at the lazy, sun-drowsed cattle.

Cotton rode back to camp and spoke briefly to Stacey and Joe. Their faces, too, reflected incredulity for a second, and then the sense hit them. Of course the damned banker could afford a bottle of whisky to scare these troublesome cows clear back to Texas.

"Hot damn!" Stacey grinned in anticipation.

In a minute they had their mounts and were off to help move the herd southwest to safety.

The maneuver took only two hours, and by suppertime the bedground was changed, though the camp stayed as it was. Kelly had his cookfire going, and Cotton sent Juan up to the knob to build a little blaze like an eye open all night up there. Them that'd come would be nervous, beginners in the stampeding business, not knowing the havoc and death such a move could cause. They'd be nervous of that fiery eye on the knob and stay clear, same as they would the camp. They'd think to come on the herd, but it wouldn't be there. Wouldn't be anything, only an eye on the hill, and the cookfire of camp.

Pearly dark came slowly over the purple plains, and the looping cooing of turtle doves slowly faded away. Juan kept up his little fire on the knob, and the serenity of the endless land with its big, fading sky seemed too sweet a confection to go sour.

A sickle moon came up on the banks of sparkling stars, putting out just enough light to see shapes of cows, horses, men.

Quietly, Cotton kept them settled, even while Cass was singing and making a circle around an imaginary herd of steers to the east.

Whoever intended to spook them off was going to get a surprise.

It sounded like such a crazy premonition that Cotton wondered if maybe he'd been stopping too much sun this past couple months. Hell, in Texas you could leave cows out a year or so and nobody'd bother 'em, but you drive 'em north awhile and all of a sudden a man becomes something else. Cows don't change. Weather don't change, ground don't change.

But the man changes. Smells money, smells fear or greed, smells power.

Got to stop it. Turn it off.

While Cass hymned to the empty pasture, Ardie hunkered down in a buffalo wallow alongside Wash. Neither spoke for fear of giving the game away. Spotted through the area where the herd had been, the rest of the hands waited alertly, hungering for a smoke.

Nearby the big black paced silently, carrying Cotton. Cotton's eyes were glowing brighter than the rind of the moon above. Dressed all in black, he was a shadow as resplendent and massive as Satan himself.

He breathed a little easier after midnight. Before that he'd feared a mob of men, maybe half the town would be out for fun and profit and free beef, but after midnight they'd be skulkers. They'd be snaking through the grass. Not a bluff and half-drunk crowd hard as hell to handle.

These would be scared. Be sneakin' through the long grass with goose guns. Be brave as hell back in town in the morning if it was to come out right for them.

The stars wheeled over the sleeping prairie. The milky way foamed with light like froth on a pail of fresh milk.

The quick, rickety bark of a coyote sounded across the dark land. One, two, three. And once more the same coughing signal rasped the velvet night.

That was it. Came from east. Was Joe Benns. Seen 'em.

Cotton grinned as the suspense and weary waiting fell away. He walked the black toward the mound of earth from which Joe had played the coyote.

132

Fiddle had cried and the dance was begun. All you had to do was find your pardner now and stomp him to death.

The others would be moving now, cussing silently, but ready.

Joe's job was to stay put, cut 'em off if they tried to get out.

Cotton would join him from the south. He hit his point like a black cat setting after a wood rat. Once in line with Joe, they were in his bag and he was holding the drawstring. He settled his Colt in his hand and turned to come up close.

A movement to his right. He held steady until a figure on a claybank horse he knew well moved in close. Cotton lowered the six-gun and waited.

"They's afoot," Joe said under his breath.

Cotton couldn't believe it for a second, but there was no reason to doubt Joe's eyes or good sense.

"Three of 'em. Left their wagon back at the coulee. Ain't no more'n that. Least on this end," Joe added, answering the unspoken question.

Could be others going to splatter in from the west and north, but there'd been no signal. No coyotes barking or owls hooting off that way tonight.

"Let's pick 'em up," Cotton said. "Don't crowd 'em into gunplay."

Joe nodded and the two of them separated and patrolled on west until Cotton caught sight of three blacker than darkness silhouettes.

"You gents are covered from clear around," Cotton said clearly, keeping his voice peaceable, like he was trying to talk a man-killing stud into behaving. "Just stay put there a second and there won't be any harm come to you."

"We quit, mister!" one of them yelled, at the same time flopping into the deep grass.

Cotton dived off headfirst as the big shotgun exploded, sending a bucket of balls right where he'd been. A pistol spoke, a quick flash. Just once. One of the boys from the west. The grass wasn't much protection from a forty-five caliber slug. The man with the greener groaned like a sick pig.

The other two had their hands kited high so's you could see the paleness waving away at them like cottonwood branches.

"Don't shoot, mister!"

Cotton had already rolled in close enough to find the downed one. Hoarse in the windpipe and bubbles making it worse. Get the shotgun first. Don't take much to touch off the far barrel.

The steel showed in the starlight, and Cotton twisted it aside and jerked hard. It came free with no resistance. Whoever was the owner wasn't interested anymore.

The breathing bubbled out. Cotton heard a little tight squeal come out of the hunched-up figure and then quiet. Cotton turned toward the other two men already surrounded and disarmed by the crew.

"Take 'em yonder to Juan's fire," Cotton said tiredly, breaking the two bore, kicking out the live shell and tossing it next to the still figure slowly cooling, slowly flexing loose.

Ardie brought up the black. "How come you didn't believe him?" Ardie teased.

"Couldn't see his eyes," Cotton said. "You bust him?"

"Yeah," Ardie said. "I couldn't see good enough to miss."

"Thanks," Cotton said. "He had an extra barrel ready."

In the light of the fire Cotton was surprised to see a fat, soft-handed shopkeeper from the cut of his coat, and the other was hardly more than a boy.

"Your son?" he asked the man.

"My nephew," the shopkeeper said, and, drawing courage from the fact that he was still alive and in firelight, added in a firm tone, "You have no right dragging us up here."

"Maybe," Cotton said, "but how would we know you was law-abiding citizens trespassin' across our herd ground?"

"Where—" the shopkeeper started to ask, puzzled, then clamping his jaw shut.

"The herd? The herd has rights, too," Cotton said. "And I'm lookin' after 'em. Now, let's get to you."

Cotton watched the younger one, a tousle-headed youngster who didn't know beans from a bull's foot.

"What were you going to make for this night's work, son?"

"Two bits," the boy said.

Joe Benns growled in the back of his throat. But he waited for Cotton to go ahead.

"That's a nice sum of money in these hard times," Cotton said sympathetically. "Too bad you couldn't have earned it."

"Yessir," the boy said. "We wasn't meanin' to hurt nobody."

"No, just ruin about five ranches in Texas and ten cowboys in Kansas," Ardie murmured, looking at the fire, uncaring now about any of it. Far as he cared, these two was as low a mutt as you could cut out of dog alley.

"You must be related to Mr. Oglethorpe," Cotton said.

"No, sir," the shopkeeper said, "we're just business acquaintances."

"I see," Cotton said. "You owe him a little money."

"Me and everybody else in town, but he hasn't foreclosed anybody yet."

"Got plenty gold in the vault probably," Cotton said. "He doesn't need more property."

"That's about the size of it," the man replied.

Cotton's easy, gentle way was reaching into the storekeeper's own sense of humanity. For sure nobody was beating him over the head nor burning the soles of his feet.

"Hard times everywhere," Cotton said. "You probably can't sell axe handles for hard money, and we can't sell cows either."

"That's the truth. I deal in bolt goods mostly, but about all you can get for calico now is a settin' of eggs. And eggs ain't worth nothin'. I got eggs runnin' out my back door."

"By golly, we haven't had an egg since we crossed the Arkansas." Cotton smiled. "Maybe we can make you a swap."

"I'll give you all you want." The shopkeeper beamed. "Just as soon as we get back home, I'll load you up with henfruit."

"Sure now, we mean to travel your way come daylight," Cotton said.

"Best not," the boy said. "They's all goin' to back Mr. Oglethorpe."

"Shut up, Buddy," the shopkeeper said. "They's been talk, but nobody knows nothin' for sure."

"You mean folks in town are likely to take up arms against us if we ride in?"

"It's possible, but I just don't think they really would." The man was trying to pass it off as a bad dream. "Shucks, why would they want to fight with you all?"

"I'd like to know," Cotton said. "Seems they'd like us drovers. I mean, when we sell the herd, they'd just smile big as bullfrogs, and we'd be glad to share out our money for a few simple pleasures."

"We figured you are goin' to exterminate Abilene. That's what Oglethorpe and Tosh are sayin'. They said you was mighty upwrought at northerners."

"Sure now," Cotton said, "and this boy was offered two bits, and you were to get an extension on your note, and that gent resting there in the grass, he was goin' to preserve something for somebody else, too."

"I don't follow you," the man said, licking his upper lip.

"Just that the banker is using you and Tosh and bald-faced boys and a whole town to put us down. He sets you against us, and keeps the gravy for his own self. Trouble is, he doesn't know right is right, and folks are human after all."

"Yessir."

"Like you ought to be with us, instead of against us. I mean, you are the folks making the banker rich. He isn't making you rich. You can see that, can't you?"

"Yes, I can see that," the man said, "but of course he risks his money."

"He doesn't really risk it because he can set you against me, or a town against another town, and it all flows like gravy back to him, you see?"

The man politely nodded, and Cotton decided even if it couldn't be done, he'd still try.

"Understand, if you just turned around to him and said, 'Look here, Mr. Banker, it's extra hard times. You boys with the money brought it on, not us that do the work. So you just get your hooks loose from us before we kill you and burn down your shack.' See? They make these credit and cash games, and folks like you and us, workin' folks, have to pay for it. Our children have to go barefoot and maybe hungry for it. Widows lose their ranches for it. Men like us lose a lifetime's labor account of it. See it?"

"I guess so."

Cotton looked at the youth. Maybe he could understand it because his mind wasn't so fixed on the idea that bankers were sacred.

"See it, son?"

"Sounds like you have something there. Two bits wouldn'ta bothered Mr. Oglethorpe's bank none, but would sure have raised Cain with your work if we'da done what we was 'sposed to do."

"Now, Buddy—" the storekeeper said.

The boy lapsed into thoughtful silence.

"So, mister, you tell the good folks of Abilene how we don't bear grudges and don't want their property, just our own money. Can you tell them? Persuade them to stay home? Put their fowling pieces aside? That's all. We believe right is right, like everybody else does."

The shopkeeper stared full into Cotton's sunburned, wind-eroded face. He couldn't believe anyone was that simple.

"Get going. Take your pardner, too. Our drive'll be down main street before noon."

"Yessir," the storekeeper stammered, and grabbed the youth by a tattered shirttail and dragged him out of the firelight and down the hill.

"You're giving them every chance to bushwhack us," Stacey said. "Why not just teach 'em some manners they won't forget?"

"I told him fair and square."

"He's a toad," Ardie said. "He'll sell us out for a whiff off the hind end of that banker."

"If they go against us, it won't be because we lied."

"I'd have given 'em a lesson in lead poisoning," Stacey said.

"Might as well get an hour's sleep." Cotton didn't want to argue. "Be dawn soon, and we'll end up this little journey north."

12

The stars still sparkled when Cotton stirred from the scant cover of his blanket. He'd allowed himself the luxury of sleeping with his boots off, and it took him a minute of blurred recollection to remember to put them on again before hopping off into the brush.

Kelly had already set a new pot of coffee next to the fire and was frying up corn dodgers and sidemeat for breakfast. When he saw Cotton come out of his blankets, he sang out loudly, "Good mornin', boss!" which sounded like a bugle blowing reveille in the quiet, pure morning.

"Good mornin'!" Ardie bellered against his saddle seat hard as a walnut rifle stock. "Good mornin', world! Good mornin', Maybelle! Here I am, ready for the hammer and the an-vil!"

The boys ate fast and went through their motions same as they had all along. A couple went out to relieve the nighthawks, the rest picked out their best horses.

Cotton hunkered a moment by the cookfire, a cup of steaming java warming through the calluses on his big hands. He tried to think of what he had to do no matter what anybody else did. Chances were those folks in town were going to bar their doors and pull the shutters and hope to hell these cowboys would disappear into a simple bad dream. That'd be all right. Cotton, if he had his druthers, might like to bare his teeth and howl and tear up the railhead for the pure joy of it, but there were too many folks down home depending on him to keep his head, and the boys', too.

"Drive them in slow and easy, Ardie," Cotton said, making sure that Ardie knew what he meant. "Give the townsfolk plenty of warning we're on our way."

"S'pose they fort up with buffalo rifles?"

"Hope they don't," Cotton said. "Just figure they're like a two-year-old colt that hasn't ever had a blanket on his back. Come in slow, slow and easy, and maybe he won't rear back and knock your ears off."

"Maybelle, get ready to duck." Ardie smiled and set off toward the herd.

In a few minutes the leaders were moseying on east as if they'd figured the way out all by themselves. The riders took their places as they had so many times before. Point, swing, flank, and drag. Remuda and chuckwagon to the rear, and Cotton off on scout. They seemed like a heavy trail of ants from high up on the knob, red, brindly, black ants moving and feeding on east, the tallow fat glistening through their summer coats.

In the far distance a little smoky haze and a glitter of tin. On west were other herds waiting it out, hoping for the bankers to let loose of the money. Might as well hope to milk a steer, Cotton thought, keeping alert. Never know.

He rode his best claybank stud. Juan had managed to roach out his tail and mane neatly and brush him down good, so he looked like a million dollars in the morning. Long-legged and deep-chested, shining solid gray-brown, his fine, broad head lifted up as proud and smart as any horse you'd ever see.

By the time the sun cleared the eastern pancake horizon, they could see the rectangular, unnatural shapes of the shipping town outlined on the flat land. The cattle moved placidly, heavy and content. Their feet were sound, their aches and pains limited to digestion, and they were more pleased than not to stroll the few miles of a fresh morning toward the long pens made of railroad ties and timbers, so new as to not yet be painted railroad red.

Cotton rode along tall and easy on the slicked-up horse, trying not to let the worry in his mind show, but he gritted his teeth, trying to figure out how he could keep right right and still keep the law. By damn it, law was law and right was right! Maybe the only way to keep right right was to take a bite off the hind end of the law just to serve notice it better do the job.

'Course, if the banker keeps his promise, he might lose some money, but it won't break him because he's pickin' up faith and trust all the time he keeps his word, and that means credit, and credit is money.

Old grulla John grazed along ahead, just managing to keep a step ahead of his mates with hardly any pressure to move on.

His eyes were always peeled, never letting anybody get too close to him. He'd grab off a great thatch of blue stem and toss his head around as he swallered it down, and glare and let his head move back to the grass again, taking a kind of sidling step as he went. Wouldn't be long he'd be looking for a drink of water to top off his appetite.

The boys all carried revolvers, and their gun belts were full of cartridges, and some carried a few extras in their shirt pockets. Laconic, weathered, rangy-eyed men as tough as old grulla John. Wanting nobody pissin' on 'em. Wanting their just due, then to hell with it, blow it all back again, just being simple, natural humans trained up into as much of a physical person as you could find.

A horse could toss one into a cactus and he'd come out ruefully smiling, figuring he should have stuck to the horse.

That's the kind they were, taking a slow walk over toward little Abilene, where the townspeople were trying to act like nature wasn't really right there on their front doorstep or right there in the main street where they'd planted alfalfa, hoping to keep the dust down.

Could see the water tower next to the tracks and close to the pens. Could see the new shingled church steeple poking up to the bright morning.

Saloons and cribs back off across the line from church and city jail. Boys could sure use some of that. Been dreamin' on it a thousand miles or so.

Rider heading out their way. Sets solid. Brass on the shirt. Right on time. Made a point of coming out alone. Looked brave, too, and dedicated to duty. Law's law.

"Mornin', Marshal."

"What you aimin' to do with them critters?"

"Goin' to put 'em in the railroad pens and ship 'em to Chicago."

"S'posin' nobody wants 'em?"

"Do I look worried?"

"No, you don't. You look like you don't know bullets from birdshot."

"You're welcome to ride along with us. We don't want to harm any private property, or hurt your town any."

"Sure glad of that, as the citizens are some sorry about losin' the harness maker last night."

"Why would a harness maker ride all the way out to our camp just to die? Shucks, I like harness makers some better'n marshals, and I need 'em both."

"Maybe he was afraid your crew'd massacre the town."

"Yes," Cotton said, "I can see that. I reckon the town is livin' close to a scream."

Almost noontime and nobody out. Old grulla John coming down the middle of the street, snatching at the sweet alfalfa patches, but snorting and rolling his eyes at the new buildings and tents and lean-tos. All you could see was eyes through the cracks and the little windows. Even the girls in the cribs were hiding out.

Somebody held a hard rod over this town to do that.

The herd lined out, coming in comfortable and slow, aiming down the street, smelling water or an end to the trail, a destination, a rendezvous, sensing that this was what they had been born and bred and traveled so far to do, and there it was, the two-by-eight timbers spiked to the six-by-eight posts. Hardly finished before money was stopped and the carpenters laid off and sent on down the track.

144

The riders looked smart. The beeves bellowing as they crowded down the street. Cotton rode ahead to the tally gate, leaving the marshal to make up his mind whether to come along or stay back and sulk.

Ardie was already there with the tally and book, making sure each herd owner would get every penny he was due, and each drover his pay.

Cotton climbed up alongside Ardie and nodded to Cass Curry at the lead. The gate was open and in they came. First off was old grulla John, branded Lazy B. Widow Dickinson's property. They had to come through from the big pen through a single walk chute into the regular shipping pens at about twenty a minute, just fast enough so no time was wasted. In three hours they tallied every one, and found a few unbranded calves and a few strays they hadn't remembered joining the drive, strays with foreign brands they'd never heard of. The final tally came to 2038.

"Pretty good." Ardie nodded.

"Pretty good, considering we tried to run a clean drive," Cotton said.

Marshal Tosh had joined them halfway through the count but kept his peace until they were all done with the tally and the gate was swung to and pinned.

"Now you got 'em in here, what you aim to do with 'em?"

"You want 'em?" Cotton asked, smiling.

"I want an answer."

Cotton ignored him. "Throw some prairie hay out of that stack down to 'em and make sure they get water," he said to Ardie. "I'll see you later."

"Yessir," Ardie said. "Make it sooner than later, though, if you can."

Cotton climbed down from his top rail perch and

mounted the claybank. Everything was as it should be. Right on schedule. None sick or lame or blind. Good stock delivered on time, as promised.

That's all any man could ask for in these times.

He rode the hundred yards up main street to the limestone building he'd visited before. Smoky Hill National Bank. Assets $700,000.

He tied the horse at the rail and walked across the limestone slab to the steps, up the steps to the door, and into the dark room with its steel wickets and oiled pitch-pine floor.

Off to the side the door to the president's office was closed.

The bald clerk in black arm sleeves waited to greet him, delay him, cool him down. "Good morning, sir, can I help you?"

"Yessir," Cotton said to the bowed-over gnome of a man and laid the tally book on the counter. "This is the record of the herd all the way from Dickinson Ranch, Texas, to Abilene, Kansas, brands and tallies and the total. Plus the contract under which they are delivered."

The old man rubbed his bald head and blinked slowly three times. "Um . . ."

Cotton felt sure that Oglethorpe was listening and hiding behind the door.

"Maybe you should call your boss," Cotton suggested. "Just to double-check everything is exactly correct."

"Yessir." The old man nodded.

Cotton looked around. No customers. No nothing.

Been warned out, likely. Everybody setting home, trembling 'cause the barbarians were coming from Texas to steal their treasure and daughters and all.

A regulator clock ticked off the seconds.

A fly buzzed. A board creaked from warp as the old man's feet shuffled across toward the closed door.

Opening the door after a faint knock, Cotton went in. The clock ticked. Board creaked, flies buzzed, muffled words from the office, and the big iron safe by the front window was locked.

Be some job getting that thing opened if you didn't know how, Cotton thought with wonder. One thing for sure, he didn't want to ever get mixed up in a bank robbery. After rape and murder, bank robbing seemed like the worst crime you could do. You always heard that. The meanest, baddest men were bank robbers.

Oglethorpe was in his nice, sanctified office, sweating. Should he pay off his honor with good, honorable money, or should he not? And once he'd decided should he, he had to decide could he? And whatever the heck he decided, he better come out with some kind of an answer pronto.

Cotton waited another tick-tock, picked up the tally book from the counter, turned and walked loudly and carefully toward the closed door. He knocked briefly and said, "Oglethorpe, are you in there?"

Silence. Whispers. A scrape of wood. A back door? No, he wasn't pure yellow, was he?

He wouldn't just run and leave all the deciding up to Cotton?

The door opened and the shiny-headed clerk came out sidewise. He kept the door closed so Cotton couldn't see in, sidling out like an Arizona sidewinder coming out a slit in a rock.

His eyes settled on Cotton's kneecaps. "Sir," he tried to say in a coarse whisper, and on the third time it coughed out, *"Sir!"*

"I'm here," Cotton said evenly. "Waiting patient as punkin pie."

"Mr. Oglethorpe suggests you return in about one hour, please." The clerk's voice couldn't come to even keel. He seemed like a horse strangling on its tongue.

Cotton kicked the door a wallop with the heel of his boot. The clerk jumped like a grasshopper and the door sprang inward, revealing the big oak rolltop desk, a couple of chairs, and nothing else excepting a back door that opened onto the side street.

Cotton set his jaw, thinking it was going to be a hard horse to break, but break him he would, and spoke gently to the trembling old man. "Don't get yourself all into a duckbath, old-timer, steady down. You just carry on and tell Oglethorpe I'll call on him in an hour." He glanced at the regulator tick-tocking the interest rates each minute, twelve percent, twelve percent, one percent per month. Compounded semi-annual.

"That'll make it just right on three o'clock. Plenty of time to do our business."

Carrying the tally book, Cotton walked out the front door and down the steps to the hitchrail where Ardie waited.

"He lit a shuck," Cotton said.

"Want us to fetch him?"

"Not yet. I don't want bloodshed. You can't ever draw back from it."

"Boys are set and ready anytime you say."

"I know, Ardie, but it don't just settle the cow to kill her."

Cotton looked slowly up and down the empty, silent street. Somewhere in the town folks were meeting; somewhere Oglethorpe was trying to persuade them that they should help him save his money and to hell with these hairy southern Texican low-lifers, or worse.

Cotton could imagine how that meeting would go once Oglethorpe started playing on the townfolk's prejudices. Johnny Rebs, carrying guns, unwashed and unshaved. Never mentioning that the war was over, that they carried six-guns for self-defense against rattlers, wild bulls, or rustlers, and they'd all be glad to take a hot bath and attend the barber if the banker would just give them their due. He'd say they was nigger lovers and their wives and daughters weren't safe because they traveled and worked together with Wash and Kelly and nobody thought nothin' about it. And God knows how he'd throw Juan in as a natural enemy. Half Injun maybe, redskin, scalp you in your sleep.

Gazing at the vacant main street, Cotton was thinking that if about ten northerners rode into San Antonio after weeks of battling sand and centipedes, what would the good, settled Texans think about them?

Too much blood had run before Cotton's eyes in the war. Too much. Too damned much, and all wasted. There were eight men dead since they'd left Texas just to get the damned beef to here. There were men in this town with wives and little children to raise. Those children were going to need their dads. Those children would carry a grudge all their lives against Texas if he should cause the death today of one of those dads.

Cotton was peaceable. More than peaceable, he was dead set against killing ordinary innocent people.

Yet right was right. And the people back home were just ordinary, innocent folks too, who were going to have to barefoot it on west if they were cheated.

Much as Cotton wanted to cross that street and drag

Oglethorpe out by his ear, he held back. Was no doubt he could do it. Question was, could he do it and not get any of his boys shot for the bravado?

"C'mon, Ardie," Cotton said, swinging up on the claybank. "We got to pow-wow."

Ardie nodded, waited to make sure a moment that nobody was going to try a backshot, and then swung up and followed along, keeping his own body in between the town and Cotton's broad shoulders.

The crew was loafing, teasing ant lions, chewing straws, and dozing like a band of dirty, bearded, ragged pirates around the chuckwagon. God knows, if you didn't know them, you'd just naturally be scared of them, so wolfy they looked.

They tensed up some when Cotton dismounted. Juan started to lead the claybank off, but Cotton said, "Just a second, Juan, we're goin' to have a meetin' and vote. All of us."

"What's up, boss?" Joe Benns asked, just to give him a way to go.

"Seems Oglethorpe wants an hour. But I'm thinking he means to make a scrap of it. He knows we delivered the cows, knows what comes next. That's the money. His bank is in between a rock and a hard place. He either pays or moves."

"We'll fight," Stacey said, his pale eyes shining like new silver dimes.

"Maybe," Cotton said softly, "but let's not just start clawing at the belly just yet. First off, I'd like everybody to tell me if he wants in or wants out. I mean, it's likely going to be a scrap. Anybody can quit now. I mean it, and no hard feelings, and I'll pay you off like before. If anybody gets hurt, he gets hurt because he made his own bet, not because I tolled him into it."

"Boss, we ain't exactly drop calves anymore," Joe said. "We can make up our minds."

"It's each mind I'm thinkin' of. A man always dies all alone."

His gaze settled on each face: Ardie's laughing nod; Stacey's young, fiery nod; Kelly's saying "Yessir," and meaning it as much as you can mean anything; Cass spitting on the ground as if he was an automatic yes and didn't want to palaver about it; Joe saying "Sure"; Wash Washington nodding; little shy Chip holding up his hand; and lastly, Juan making that little eye squinch, same as you touch a horse with your knee, it says everything needs to be said; and that was the vote.

"All right. It's all the way," Cotton said. "Now I'm saying we're off our range, and there's no help. So if we're goin' to fight, let's have a plan to get back home on."

The boys hadn't thought that far. Sure, just pull your hogleg, shoot somebody, take the money and ride home on velvet. Cotton knew, though, that once it happened, you were outlawed and fair game. They'd all have a price on their heads, and they'd all be hounded by posses all the way south to the Nations and by the Pinkerton undercover agents after that.

"First thing, we better set a meeting place for after the dust settles, like if somebody gets separated or has to split off."

Ardie nodded. "Could happen. One man alone would get torn to pieces by the pack."

"So, no matter what happens," Cotton said, "we are all going to meet at the fork of the trail and the Smoky Hill River. Understood? We don't leave there till we're all together, or we all come back for them as hasn't been able to make it."

"'Course if you're dead, we ain't comin' back." Ardie laughed.

"Same for you." Cass grinned.

"Me!" Ardie frowned. "Me dead? Maybelle, you hear that?"

"We're talkin' about if somebody's treed, or in jail, or some such, we come back. Otherwise we keep travelin'."

"We takin' the chuckwagon?" Kelly asked.

"No," Cotton said. "We ride our best horses and lead along all we can. Juan's main job will be to keep us in horses."

"No!" Juan protested.

"Look, Juan, we got all kinds of fire eaters, but nobody knows how to manage horses like you."

"So, let's go get our money." Stacey stood up eagerly.

"Wait a second." Cotton held up his hand. "Now's when we need to use our heads."

"I'm listening," Ardie said.

"There's a main street and a cross street. The bank is at the cross. The saloon is catty-cornered. General store is straight across. Church on the other corner. That's four good spots for riflemen to bushwhack us."

"Not in a church," Stacey said.

"We don't take a chance," Cotton said. "Now, each one of them buildings has to be flanked and taken before I go in the bank. Otherwise those boys might chop us into hogmeat with their rifles."

They nodded and smiled, feeling better. Before they'd figured somebody was certain to get hit, now they saw a chance of a good plan saving all of them.

"I'm betting Oglethorpe'll be in the bank. He'll be trying to get our backs set up for the cross fire. But nobody goes in there except me."

"Why?" Stacey frowned.

"Because I don't want to worry about somebody losing his head."

Stacey remembered the Mexican horse thieves and set his jaw bitterly.

"Now, catty-cornered is the saloon. Be some brave ones in there liquored up. I have in mind that Ardie, Chip, and Joe sort of sidle in there from the front and order a drink and not drink it till right on three o'clock. Now Juan will have the riding horses moved up behind the saloon and can back 'em up."

He saw that each understood his intentions. "Stacey, looks like you automatically picked the church. If nothing else, you'll learn something about Christians. Wash'll lead in, and, if necessary, Wash'll shoot first; be sure you follow his lead. That leaves Kelly to shine his teeth at the General Mercantile with Cass."

Stacey clamped his jaws together and looked away to hide his anger.

"Everybody just goes in the front doors?" Ardie asked.

"No. You and Chip and Joe go in the front door of the Daffodil, but Juan will be in the back. Wash and Stacey have to get into the church, probably by the back because the front door will be barred. And I reckon Kelly can go in the front of the Mercantile, but Cass come in the back. Settled?"

"I can't think of anything better," Ardie said.

Joe and Cass nodded. Wash smiled. Chip looked worried.

"Where's Tosh goin' to be?" Stacey asked. "I want him."

"This ain't your show, Stacey," Cotton growled. "You mind and follow orders."

"My guess is he'll be in the bank," Cass put in.

"He's the joker in the deck," Joe said.

"So we all look for him, and once somebody eyeballs him, don't let him loose," Ardie said.

"If he's hid out in the bank," Stacey persisted, "that's two against one."

Cotton thought about it. "Remember, we aren't tryin' to be heroes. All we want is our money. No more'n that. So if I see he's in the bank with Ogle-thorpe, I'll come out and ask somebody to come back in with me. There's no iron schedule."

"S'pose they don't let you out?"

"One of you is goin' to be loose. I mean once you size up the setup, you can see. Might be like Stacey says, nobody'll be in the church. Then he can come right over to the bank.

"Anything else?"

"S'posin' they drag out and start cuttin' wads before we even get to three o'clock?"

"Then that's the levee bustin'," Cotton said. "I tell you this, I aim to take what we earned, and we're goin' to do our damnedest to get outta here without blood-shed. Right?"

They all understood and agreed to it.

Stacey licked his lips. Cotton thought if it came to gunplay, Stacey'd get over that buck fever. Hard thing would be to stop him once he got started, and that was something else again. Another cloud on the horizon. Might as well say it.

"Look, we're not robbin' a bank. We're takin' our own money. If anybody ever gets an idea of bein' a bank robber out of this, I'm goin' to join the first posse after him. Understand?"

They didn't bother to nod. Knowing him, they knew what he meant.

"Anybody got the time?"

Kelly pulled his nickel-plated turnip out and said, "Quarter till three, boss."

Cotton thought about the horses again. If he was being really farsighted, he'd have Juan leading a string of spare mounts off toward the ford, but Juan was needed for his cool head.

"Boss, I made a friend here," Juan said, sensing the problem. "He's a Mexican kid. I was just talkin' to him. He don't have a family. I gave him an old rope he could trade for beans."

"How old is he?" Cotton asked.

"Old enough," Juan said. "Let me get him."

Cotton nodded, and Juan disappeared behind the haystack and returned leading a thin, almost emaciated youth dressed in rags, barefoot, shaggy-haired, but clean and bright-eyed.

"Is he honest?" Cotton asked Juan.

"His name is Jesus." Juan smiled.

"Can you go on a trip?" Cotton asked the wide-eyed boy.

Jesus nodded.

"I'll pay you something. You may want to go on."

"I want to go to New Mexico," the boy said. "My mother is in Albuquerque."

"You know where the big trail crosses the Smoky Hill?"

"True. About fifteen miles southwest."

Cotton appreciated the assuredness, the unafraid attitude.

"Okay, you'll start right now with a dozen horses. Juan, you set him up. The rest of you pick out your next best horse for him. I want my black stud. I'll ride the claybank."

Juan nodded, and in a few minutes the extra horses were ready and Jesus was up on a good, steady sorrel gelding and given a few words of last advice.

Cotton watched the preparation, making doubly sure the boy was the right one and would do. Once in a while you come across a natural hand, and this young man looked right. He'd be waiting, and they'd ride the river together.

Cotton held off until Jesus had the lead rope secured to his saddle horn. The big gelding would keep them gentle, and they sure as hell wouldn't drag him.

Cotton didn't add to the advice Juan had given in Spanish; he simply stood beside Juan and said, "You wait at the crossing. If nobody turns up by morning, you do whatever you feel like."

"Yessir."

The boy kicked bare heels into the gelding's ribs and led the string of horses out the lower end of town. Nothing hidden. They weren't thieves in the night. They were just doing a job the only way they knew how and weren't ashamed of it. Cotton felt better after seeing the boy, because Juan was freed, and he was a deadly Yaqui Indian if he needed to be.

"Soon as you know the saloon is settled," Cotton told Juan, "come right on over to side me in the bank."

Juan's smile reminded Cotton of a hungry gila monster.

The men checked their guns. Kelly looked at his watch.

"Three o'clock, boss."

"Let's go. Two at a time. Just gentle and easy. Treat the whole town like a two-year-old colt never been touched by a man before. Speak low and don't crowd him."

They knew. No sense telling them again.

Ardie, Chip, and Joe drifted off, with a dollar between them, aiming up the street for the saloon, their horses swinging their hooves in a frolicky walk. Cotton nodded to Juan, who rode in a different direction, would circle like a lost cowhand, end up in the alley by the beer barrels stacked behind the corner saloon.

He nodded to Cass and Kelly. Kelly jammed a pearl-handled six-gun into his waist, mounted up his fast mule and, looking like a giant African, rode along with Cass toward the Mercantile. Couple foreigners looking for cheese and crackers. Soon as they were well away, Cotton gave the word to Stacey and Wash.

"Say a prayer for all of us," he said.

Wash smiled. "We goin' to be all right, boss, don't worry."

"Okay, Wash," Cotton said, not feeling all that encouraged. Hell of a thing to have to endanger your people just to get your due wage.

13

Cotton was alone, his forty-four clean, oiled, and loaded. He topped the claybank, took a deep breath and said his own prayer under his breath. He felt he was the only one of the bunch who really knew what this town could do to them, and he was pretty sure it was already setting up to try.

Well, all right, deal the cards!

He gave the stud a knee and drifted up main street, a simple man going to conclude a business deal with the banker. Ordinarily he would just pick up a certified check and ride on, but this time the banker would have to pay off in cash money.

Horses stood cant-legged at the hitchrail. Town still quiet. Farmers warned away. Children in the storm cellars. Eyes peeking here and there. Well. Who's to blame? Sure not the Texans.

He tied a snap loop to the hitchrail and carried his empty saddlebags over his left arm. He was afraid the door would be locked. It would have been such a simple way to thwart him, but no, it was wide open, and they were going to be clever instead of simple. Deal the cards to the clever players.

The old clerk was perched on his stool behind his wicket, attempting to add a column of figures in a ledger, but Cotton saw the gray sweat on his bald head. First things first.

As the old man looked up, Cotton said, "Give me the gun. You don't need it."

"Yessir," the clerk said, lifting the ledger, revealing a little thirty-two centerfire. Cotton pocketed the piece.

In the Daffodil saloon Joe and Ardie stood at the bar, beers next to their elbows, watching the silent and grudging knot of men, all heavily armed. Townsmen, drunks, a couple farmers, the saloon owner and the bartender, all pretending they were something else, but they were all sweating that grayness that came out of fear and hate instead of the humidity.

"Times was," Ardie was saying, "I come into a place and we was a jolly bunch of buckaroos swinging the girls and swiggin' down the drinks."

"I recollect," Joe said solidly. "Seems like the time's changed."

"Well, they's seven of them and three of us, Joe. That seems the way they dance nowadays."

"I don't get your meaning, cowboy," the grizzled, red-nosed saloonkeeper said.

Ardie drew his old Colt and laid his hand on the bar so the barrel aimed right at the saloonkeeper's middle.

"I mean the first customer that objects is goin' to cause the untimely end of our red-nosed bar dog." Ardie laughed.

The others in the saloon turned slowly. It was too

easy. They looked from Ardie and the big revolver over their shoulders to where Joe was leaning against the wall. He seemed to be polishing the sight of his six-gun on the sleeve of his shirt. It moved back and forth, back and forth. Chip stood in the other corner, half hidden behind a beaded curtain.

They'd been had, knew it, knew they were suckered in cold before they'd even got settled as to what they meant to do.

"Easy, Tex. You can put them guns away." The saloonkeeper tried to hold up his end of it, but his voice was lifeless. There was nobody in this room would draw against a gun aimed right at his heart.

"Anybody know a good joke?" Ardie asked, smiling.

Juan came silently in through the back door, looked over the scene, nodded and went on out the front.

In the Mercantile, Kelly was keeping the little round German busy ordering peppermints and dried peaches and salt herring. While Cass seemed to be just looking as he wandered up and down the back aisle of boots and beans and bear traps, always staying toward the rear, behind the others in the store who seemed to be a lot more nervous than the usual cracker-barrel loafers. The three gents setting on sacks of oats had guns strapped on. One old geezer had his rifle leaning on his knee. He was just setting there looking stupid. What the hell good was the rifle if there was a hostile man with a short gun behind you?

Kelly walked by him, bumped the rifle and said, "Excuse me," reached down his big hand, took the stock and lifted it away from the frustrated, trembling old man.

"Say, ain't that a nice old bushwhacker," Kelly said,

pushing a peppermint stick down the barrel and laying the rifle on the counter out of reach of its owner.

"Never mind," the red-faced German said. "What else you want?"

"More licorice whips"—Kelly made his crocodile smile—"about ten bags."

Four apple knockers there in the store and two Texans who knew their business. The storekeeper and his friends were fired up, but their purpose was vague. The marshal had just told them to get ready for a turkey shoot. He hadn't said these cowboys would get behind them, hadn't said they was big, lean, and mean as August rattlesnakes.

Wash and Stacey entered the back door of the church, coming in past the altar, walking softly through the dim, hallowed hall. It seemed reverential and holy, all silent and smelling of new lumber and furniture polish. The altar and its cloth all neat and tidy. A silver-plated crucifix of Our Lord dying in agony that all should have everlasting life. Pews lined up in front of the altar, and at the front windows, four men crouched with rifles and shotguns.

Young Stacey shuddered, his innocent faith shattered. He just couldn't believe it, but Wash had a gun in each hand. He'd expected it, and knew Stacey was going to need a few seconds to understand that God's house was also a house belonging to the money changers.

The men were on their knees peeking out the curtained windows raised high enough for simple bushwhacking.

"Can we pray with you, gents?" Wash said softly into the heavy, holy room.

The men scrambled, looked over their shoulders, and seeing the two gun man backed up by another, decided to reexamine the state of their souls.

"Maybe you gents'd rather pray over here at the altar," Wash suggested.

The men moved. One of them, an old lanky, bearded prophet with hollow cheeks and deep-set eyes said, "Peace be unto you, brother."

"Likewise," Wash said, keeping his two guns steady. He made sure they faced the crucified Christ. "Anybody got a few words?"

"Lord God in heaven, Our Redeemer, we beseech thee to turn aside the assaults of the Nubians," the old prophet prayed. "We plead for peace, and we pray for the souls of the damned who live by the sword and must therefore perish . . ."

Wash smiled.

Stacey was back on top of it again, recovered from the hypocrisy that had sickened him. These men were first enemies; secondly they were Christian brethren.

Saloon, store, church, bank.

Cotton spoke to the old man. "Bring out Oglethorpe, please, and anybody else in there."

"Yessir."

The gnome squirreled off to the private office and disappeared. In a moment Oglethorpe emerged with the clerk.

"Yes," he said, "how do you do, Mr. Dunbar?" He tried to smile, tried to carry it off as if it wasn't happening.

"I brought you the tally book. They're your cows now, delivered as promised, fat and sound. Two thousand and thirty-eight."

Cotton placed the worn, linen-covered tally book on the counter.

"I figure that is exactly $67,254."

"A lot of money." Oglethorpe smiled stiffly.

"In a way, but divided up amongst six ranchers who've worked years for it, it don't seem so much, especially as it is all goin' to pay off their back mortgages, including interest."

"You folks live mighty poor in Texas," Oglethorpe stalled.

"But we pull together," Cotton said. "Just put the money in my saddlebags and I'll be movin' along."

"We don't keep that kind of money here," Oglethorpe said.

"Get that money, else I'm goin' to take you to Texas to explain your default."

Through the front window Cotton could see Juan emerge from the saloon's batwings. All secure.

"I can't." Oglethorpe sighed tiredly.

"You'll open that safe and pay."

"Or?"

"Or you will ride home with us."

"You're threatening me. You mean to rob me."

"No. You're the threat, and you're the robber. Now get on with it. Right is right, and I'm done palaverin'."

Oglethorpe wasn't going to do it, Cotton suddenly realized. There was a greed in him that wasn't going to yield to words. It just wasn't. He looked so grand with his shampooed muttonchops, and his bright, confident eyes, and his nice pink jowls, looking as if he was born to be cock of the roost, and it seemed like kind of a shame to take him down.

Wasn't much choice. Even as the imperious man

163

balanced on his toes smiling, shaking his head no, confidently no, Cotton leaped like a cat and smashed the fat, tonsured cheek with his huge, scarred, dirt-grained fist. The banker spun around to one knee. Cotton brought his boot up and kicked him square in the belly.

Oglethorpe rolled aside as Cotton stepped back, bristling, sensing danger, watching the old clerk huddled in the corner.

"Open the safe," Cotton said.

Oglethorpe crawled on hands and knees to the great iron safe and started turning the dial. Cotton backed another step.

Keep your back to a wall and play out the hand.

While things were holding smoothly enough in the saloon and the Mercantile, Stacey grew increasingly more nervous.

"What's holding them up?" he asked no one as he watched the front of the bank across the street, anxiously waiting for Cotton to step outside with full saddlebags.

He watched Juan go up the steps and pass inside, and said, "That damned Juan, how come he gets into the catbird seat?"

"Steady down, Stacey," Wash said, never relaxing his vigilance over his parishioners. "We'll be outta here fast as a cut cat."

"You don't know! They might have taken Cotton prisoner in there, waiting for us to show ourselves."

"You worry too much, boy." Wash smiled.

"Don't call me boy, you—"

"Just a second, Stacey," Wash said strongly, "I'm running this shindig because the boss said so. Now calm down."

164

Stacey's eyes blazed. "You want to settle this right now? You been tryin' to topdog me ever since we cut down them Mexicans. I've got a bellyful of your uppity ways."

"Stacey, I'm ready to settle up later, but right now the boss said no gunplay. Remember?"

"Now you're callin' me stupid," Stacey snarled.

"You goin' to let a nigger talk like that to you?" the old prophet asked slyly.

"Stacey," Wash pleaded, "don't let this old buzzard turn your head. Right now we can't be bickerin' about small potatoes."

"How come they put a nigger boss over a white man?" the prophet asked deviously. "That the way they do it in Texas? That what the war was all about? Texans lost, niggers won, that what happened?"

"You shut up, old man," Wash said. "I don't want no more from you."

"He's got a point," Stacey said, pacing nervously back and forth.

"Next thing," the old bearded prophet said, "is they will be struttin' with your women . . . marryin' your sister—"

"I told you," Wash yelled, and smashed the old man on the side of the head with his six-gun.

Months before, when Stacey had filed down the sear on his six-gun to make the trigger touch off like a split red curly hair, he hadn't known that it would go off like that. It didn't seem he even touched it, that it was the force of his fear and anger and hatred that set it off, that it was his knotted emotions twisted so strong, making the six-gun go off by itself. The bullet caught Wash square between the shoulders, sending him sprawling against the altar.

Of the four men there, three of them were running for the back door, the front door, anywhere away from the white-eyed boy. The revolver crashed three times, and the three unarmed men screamed. It wasn't instantaneous, they kicked and flopped like slaughtered animals, their blood spurting over the floor and against the wall, and their screams died slowly.

The prophet fell against the first pew.

The saloon felt like a steamboiler with a fire under it and no safety valve. Every minute became more compressed, more stressed. Joe watched Juan enter the bank and said, "It won't be long now."

A little boy chased a loose ball into the street and was chased down by a distraught mother who grabbed him and ran back out of sight. The whole town seemed like a mortar bomb with the fuse already smoking.

"I'd like a glass of beer," Ardie said, "and then I'm goin' to find Maybelle upstairs and we're goin' to hoot and holler the rest of the week."

No one listened. The sweat, the gray ooze out of their skins, wet the bellies of their shirts. Held prisoner, the townsmen were each trying to figure a way of escape. Any kind of a break in the silence of their captivity would spook them like wild cattle seeing a flapping yellow slicker.

The sudden cacophony of a gun blazing rapidly in the church and the howls of the dying triggered them off. The Kansans dived for cover looking for hideout guns, and in a second Ardie killed the bartender and the bar owner and leaped behind the bar for cover. Chip fell forward from the beaded curtain, a hole in his forehead, a smile on his lips. He never knew what hit him.

Joe Benns didn't know how to hide. Wasn't in his nature. Like a bull he faced the room with two six-shooters and let loose a swath of lead, knocking men sideways and catapulting them through windows, but he was too big a target to miss. In spite of Ardie's own covering fire and his yelling at Joe to join him behind the bar, Joe took a fifty-caliber slug through the throat from a buffalo gun and suddenly he was no longer Joe Benns. He wasn't anything recognizable except for arms and legs and a pair of six-shooters falling from his hands.

"You bastard!" Ardie yelled at a spade-bearded man in greasy buckskins bringing up the barrel of his Sharps fifty to bear next on Ardie himself. Ardie snapped off the first shot and broke the buffalo hunter's shoulder. His second took the top of his head off.

There were none left alive in the saloon now except Ardie. The dying groans of men were not any worse than he'd heard at Shiloh, but at Shiloh the men were armies dying for a cause.

The Mercantile exploded at the same time. In his pacing through the back of the store, Cass had found the blasting supplies in the form of coils of fuse and a keg of black powder. He had rolled the keg into the middle of the store, inserted a fuse that led to the front door where Kelly was smoking a store-bought cigar with great pleasure.

"That's a fine idea for keeping the peace." Kelly laughed. "Cass, you got a real sense of humor."

"You," Cass said to the German storekeeper, "you just set right on that keg and keep quiet."

"Ach, no . . ." the storekeeper cried, wilting under the ivory teeth shining at him from huge Kelly.

"Now the rest of you gents understand I'm goin' to blow this whole shebang sky high you start getting heroic ideas," Kelly said, addressing the three sodbusters slumped on their oat sacks, puffing up a smoke cloud from his cigar.

They nodded dismally, but there was the nervousness of an animal in a cage, playing possum but ready to dart, bite, scratch, and fly. Their guns were piled up on the front counter.

Cass happened to be passing close by the German when the terror let loose in the church and the saloon. The furious fusillade of gunfire and the hooks of pain screaming from those two buildings were too much for the German. He'd had the knife all along hid out in his left black sleeve protector. The pandemonium in the church and saloon set him off. Hearing the gunfire in the church, Cass automatically turned his blind side to the German. The knife came up through the diaphragm, just under the ribs in an upward thrust, and Cass hadn't even time to look surprised or mad. Up until then he'd been kind of laughing at the way he'd set up the keg of powder. Now he was dead.

The German scuttled for the back room, and Kelly helped him along with a bullet through the back of his bald head.

The other three gents were running, clodhoppers banging toward the back shelves, and Kelly quietly and deliberately shot each one. Finished, he looked at the drab, clay-hued face of old Cass, and said, "C'mon, old friend, I'm not goin' to leave you here."

Taking the back of Cass's leather vest, he dragged the body to the front door, paused to put the glow of his cigar to the powder fuse, then dragged Cass along with him out the front door and aimed for the bank across the street.

"Doggone it," he murmured, tears leaking from his dark eyes. "Doggone it, Cass, it ain't right."

In the bank Cotton almost had it won. He figured Tosh was in the office waiting to come busting out as Juan and him would be leaving, their backs exposed and vulnerable.

Fine! Let him stay in his hideout, just so long as everybody knew it.

Oglethorpe turned the nickel-plated handle and pulled the door open. He'd never thought it would go this far, but now that it had, he had to go along with it.

When the first shot went off in the church, Cotton knew from then on it would be a war to save what was left. The further eruption of fire from the church, and the massive gunfire from the saloon followed by the steady one, two, three, four shots in the Mercantile, meant the house of cards had fallen.

Juan went to the window. "Here comes Kelly."

Cotton turned to look, and Oglethorpe, who had been waiting for a break, yelled, "Now!" and brought out his derringer two-shooter. Marshal Tosh came out firing and leaped behind the counter.

Cotton rolled one way, Juan the other. The two-shooter missed both times, and Cotton's heavy slug threw the banker against the window, shattering the glass, his body sprawling half inside, half outside.

Cotton felt a sledgehammer smack his shoulder, spinning him to the left just as another bullet screamed by his ear.

His right hand held steady as he fired through the thin wood of the counter, bringing out a sharp groan.

Three more slugs in a six-inch triangle splintered the wood, and Cotton heard a grunt and then a wet moan. Juan darted across the floor to the end of the counter, gun in hand. His usually impassive face rumpled with a look of horror and revulsion as he saw the gut-shot Marshal kicking out his life.

"Get the money, Juan," Cotton groaned, holstering his six-gun, coming to his feet.

"You hurt bad, boss?" Juan asked as he loaded the saddlebags with packages of bank notes.

"I'm okay. Where's that clerk?"

"Here, Mr. Dunbar."

Cotton saw the little man squatting in a safe corner, his hands over his face.

"Get up here right now," Cotton said, and shoved the tally book across the counter.

"Write there on the last page 'Paid in full,' and I'll sign it."

"Yessir." The clerk came up from his crouch and wrote swiftly.

Cotton took the pen and added in big script, Cotton Dunbar, Bar D, Texas.

"That's yours," he said to the clerk. "You show it to the lawmen and the judge when they come. Okay?"

"I promise." The gnome raised his trembling right hand.

"Let's go," Cotton said. "How much?"

"Comes to $65,000 even," Juan said. "Okay?"

"Sure. Give the banker the change," Cotton said. "Let's gather up and ride."

In the street Cotton secured the bags behind his saddle with his right hand. His left arm was numbing up rapidly, blood oozing steadily down his left sleeve.

"Better hurry, boss, the store is goin' blow up in a minute," Kelly said, laying Cass's body down with his head on the step. "Cass ain't goin'."

Ardie came hobbling out of the saloon, his face blackened by gun smoke, his bandanna wrapped around his right thigh. "They're dead," he said. "All of 'em."

"Watch the horses. Move 'em around the corner."

Cotton ran to the church and burst inside.

Stacey was kneeling in front of the altar, staring at the crucifix. Cotton quickly swept around the room and saw death everywhere.

Stacey knelt as a petrified acolyte, frozen in penance, but there wasn't time for anything like that, not now, and Cotton slapped the boy once as hard as he could and caught him with a hard backhand the other way.

Cotton couldn't understand. What he saw didn't ring true. No one had a gun except lifeless Wash, who was shot in the back, and Stacey, who was a cringing idiot.

"Wake up!" Cotton commanded, and Stacey's eyes gradually cleared and his mind started fearfully working.

"What happened?"

"Let's go. I'll explain it later," Stacey mumbled.

Stacey, standing, his whole body trembling, knew what he had done.

"It don't look right, Stacey," Cotton said. "Tell me."

"They jumped Wash. That's it."

The old prophet sagging over the altar moved his hand and brought it slowly to his head before opening

171

his eyes. He stared directly at Stacey with heart-stopping accusation. "Why'd you kill him, son?"

"I didn't do it!" Stacey yelled, jammed the muzzle of his six-gun against the old prophet's head and instantly pulled the trigger.

"Outside," Cotton said sickly. "We're riding for Texas."

In the Mercantile, when the fire reached the hole, the powder keg exploded, blowing the store into flinders, every manner of merchandise from overalls to pick handles flying through the sky as well as the flimsy structure itself, the roof heading for the sky in two pieces, the walls blown outward. It seemed like Shiloh for a few moments as the concussion rocked the remaining buildings and the church shook like it had the staggers, and then there was a dusty, reverential silence.

Cotton, dragging Stacey by the arm, ran across the street to where Ardie and Kelly and Juan waited with the horses in the lee of the stone bank.

"Let's make some time!" Cotton yelled, topped the claybank and headed south.

When he felt the big horse falter, he reined the claybank down to a walk while the others caught up with him.

The price they'd paid was enough to twist his guts and drown his dreams with black bile. His shoulder ached as if it had a red hot poker in it, but it had quit bleeding.

Ardie came alongside and for once had nothing to say.

"Did we leave any of ours alive?" Cotton asked slowly.

"No, Captain. Joe and Chip were finished. You saw Wash, and Kelly brought Cass out."

"Damn, I thought I was done with war," Cotton groaned, despairing for the loss of his good men.

"Wasn't your fault. We all had a vote. There'll be a grieving in that town tonight, too."

Stacey, Kelly, and Juan walked their animals alongside now, saying nothing.

The horses' flanks were lathered and their breathing strained and hoarse.

Approaching the ford of the Smoky Hill, they felt a numbing weariness overcoming them. Their thoughts were sluggish and their bodies would hardly move.

Jesus came out of the shade of a grove of black walnuts on the sorrel and said to Juan, "This is all?"

"Yes," Juan said.

Fishing out some bills from the saddlebag, Cotton passed them over to Jesus. "There's your pay. Take the sorrel and that paint horse of Cass's and head for New Mexico pronto! There's going to be a lot of lawmen looking for us, so get clear."

"*Sí, señor,*" the youth said, and taking the lead line of the paint horse, went splashing across the river.

Cotton stopped at the river and dismounted heavily. The others followed suit.

"We'll change horses," Cotton said, "and make another fast run. We can be in the Nations come dark."

With Juan's help, he changed his saddle to the black stud and led the horse a slow circle waiting for the others.

"Ready," Ardie said.

"Not quite. I'm troubled in my mind about what

173

happened. So many good men gunned down. Why? I want to know." He looked each of the men in the eye. "I know that nobody can commit such carnage without paying for it. The Christers call it atonement. But it is just paying off the guilt."

"I don't understand," Stacey said nervously. "They're dead. That's all there is to it."

"No, there's more, because we're still alive and we owe all those dead men. We caused it someway. I don't know how. I had it planned out and foolproof, but something slipped up."

"It started in the church," Ardie said.

"I told you what happened in the church," Stacey said, backing off a step.

"The brass on the floor . . . it was all from just one gun, your forty-four."

"That don't mean anything!" Stacey cried. "Wait'll my sister hears what you're accusing me!"

"Aye," Cotton said heavily, "that's the hardest part. In all that flame and smoke I saw Penny's face looking anxious at us. I can't explain it, but I'm telling the truth."

"Oh Lordy." Kelly shut his eyes. "I don't like any ha'nts in my eyes."

"There's more, Stacey," Cotton said more calmly. "The old man with the beard accused you, and you shot him. Why?"

"Because he wanted to stir up trouble between us. That's easy to figure," Stacey said, but his voice trembled and his words came out stuttering and his washed-out eyes were going wild.

"If you killed Wash, I want you to own up to it like a man," Cotton said strongly.

Stacey took another step backward, his eyes glowing

like molten silver, his face chalk white, his hand caressing the butt of his hair-trigger forty-four.

"S'pose I did. Suppose he was uppity with me, suppose he wanted our women—"

"I knew Wash better'n that, Stacey. He was a calm, good-natured man, nothing else."

"You're sayin' he was better'n me!" Stacey's voice was shrill now. "Let me tell you, I'm better'n any goddamned nigger in Texas, and I'm plumb tired of you ridin' me all the time!"

"Don't—" Cotton tried, but Stacey's hand was pulling out the blue steel weapon and bringing it up to bear.

Like a blind snake striking, Cotton's response was completely automatic.

Stacey's hair trigger went off first, but too soon. The bullet tore the ground between the two men. Cotton's bullet an instant later took Stacey through the heart, dropping him without a sound.

A long, sick moment passed before Cotton said, "I'm sorry. I didn't want to do that."

"You had no choice," Ardie said.

"Surely he knew I could beat him." Cotton clamped his jaws and shut his eyes for a moment.

"Maybe that's what you were talking about. Paying off the guilt. He caused it and he paid it."

"That's a lot to pay," Cotton said heavily. "Tie him on a horse. I want to bury him in Texas."

"You aim to travel fast, then," Ardie said.

"That telegraph wire is already tapping out the news ahead of us. We will just keep riding and changing horses until we're home."

"Yessir, Captain," Ardie said.

Bringing the extra horses, they rode the rest of the

day, changing mounts every twenty miles. They crossed into Oklahoma territory shortly after dark and continued on down the broad, hoof-cut trail, stopping only to change horses and take a drink of water. Cotton had learned the value of speed and surprise from Stonewall Jackson, and he knew what extra strength men had if needed on a march or on a ride. By dawn they were approaching the Texas border.

Sore and tired, the horses protested, but Cotton wouldn't slow the pace. He was already a hundred miles farther along than any normal man would have been, and the posses would be searching fruitlessly way back yonder where they'd been the day before.

14

All through the next day he held the pace, never stopping to eat or feed the horses. Only water, change mounts, and then run. Water, change mounts, run, on and on, south to safety.

Maybe not safety, but to acquit himself, he had to see that money went to the right people.

Cass had no kin, his share was riding free. Better to give it to Ardie if they lived through the run.

Next day, like pale ghosts on salt-sweated horses, they cleared west of Fort Worth where the telegraph clicked away, but no one looked for them, and no one saw the tight little band hurrying on south.

At least they were in Texas, where they could get a fair trial maybe, but Cotton wasn't waiting for any lawman's hand on his shoulder. He was riding with the money. He was going to see the debts paid, and then take whatever came next.

After three days in the saddle, their thighs raw and

their horses burned out, they passed west of San Antone and Cotton slowed the pace. They were very near to home.

Cass's ranch was first in line. A couple of Mexicans and an old fur trapper cared for the place and waited for Cass to come back.

The four riders had to come slow off their mounts after they rode into the yard, their guns ready.

"Easy, boys," the old trapper said, seeing how worn they were and how their horses had been rode into the ground. "Light and stay awhile. Enrique, make some grub, hurry it up!"

They peeled out of their saddles and walked with wooden legs, like mechanical dolls, until they could feel circulation in their feet and their eyes got used to the quiet.

They were too tired to eat much, even though they'd had nothing but water and parched corn for two days.

It was better that way.

"Don't founder now that we're home," Cotton said, and slumped down on the floor with his back to the wall.

At dawn they were rested and ready to ride the last leg to the Dickinson ranch with Stacey's body shrouded in a tarpaulin.

Picking their best mounts, and explaining that Cass wasn't coming back, they left the old man and the Mexicans with whatever they could salvage. The ranch was so remote, they could probably live the rest of their lives there without anyone bothering.

Walking their horses, Cotton said, "You know the telegraph will have the federal marshals and the Texas Rangers out for us. We won't be able to just ride in and start livin' again."

"For me, Sonora is safe," Juan said.

"I can't go back to the South," Kelly said, "and I don't want to go north. Supposin' I could tag along with you, boss. I'm still a pretty good bean burner."

"We'll see," Cotton said.

"Oh Maybelle!" Ardie yelled for the first time in what seemed a week. "Why don't we just go frolickin' in sunny California!"

"Somehow we've got to get the money to the ranchers, then we're free," Cotton said.

Passing by Cotton's lonely Bar D, they went directly on over the hill to Penny Dickinson's ranch. They approached it slowly from four sides and came together at the house. There was no sign of a trap.

Penny ran outside and met them on the veranda. Spontaneously she stood on her toes, grabbed Cotton around the neck and kissed him full on the lips. "Oh, am I ever glad to see you!"

"Penny, it wasn't easy," Cotton said, noticing how Ardie was picking out lookout places to guard against surprise, while Juan and Kelly took shovels up the hill to the family plot.

Cotton brought the saddlebags of money into the kitchen and set them on the table. "There's the money that'll pay the debts."

"Damn the money, just thank heaven you're safe," she declared, her eyes brimming with tears of joy.

"Stacey's dead. I brought him back here to be buried."

"What a shame," she said, her voice catching. She lowered her head. "He was just a boy. He had his whole life ahead of him. But I'd always had a feeling he'd die young. . . ."

"There's no time. The law is after us. We pretty

nearly massacred Abilene," Cotton said. "We're on the run."

"Where can you go?"

"West till we hit an ocean, I reckon."

"We can leave the others' money with the Martin brothers," she said suddenly.

"Wait a second, Penny," Cotton said, puzzled, "we have to run, not you. You can pay off the banker and keep the ranch."

"Why would I want to do a thing like that?" She smiled and gently touched his blood-caked sleeve. "Why not keep the money and give the banker the ranch? Oh, you shy galoot!"

"Ma'am?"

"Would you leave me here to dry out like a cowhide on a fence?"

"No, ma'am," Cotton murmured, his mind moving too tiredly to keep up with her chatter. Whatever it was she wanted was fine with him. He knew that much anyway.

"We're going to California!" she declared.

"And raise cows?" he questioned wearily.

"Is that all you want?" she asked.

"No, ma'am." Cotton smiled, and with only one good arm, he couldn't have fended her off even if he'd tried.

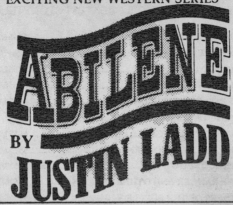